DATE DUE

OC 0 1 '08			
OC 1 8 '08			
OC 2 7 '08			
NO 2 6 '08			
DE 2 6 '08			
JA 2 2 '09			
FE 2 0 '09			
MAR 0 3 2011			

D1294267

SALSA WITH ME

SALSA WITH ME

•

Roni Denholtz

AVALON BOOKS
NEW YORK

082708

Published by Thomas Bouregy & Co., Inc.
160 Madison Avenue, New York, NY 10016

Library of Congress Cataloging-in-Publication Data

Denholtz, Roni S.
  Salsa with me / Roni Denholtz.
       p.   cm.
  ISBN 978-0-8034-9912-6 (hardcover : acid-free
paper)   1. Dance teachers—Fiction.   2. Salsa
(Dance)—Fiction.   I. Title.

  PS3554.E5314S25   2008
  813'.54—dc22   2008017327

PRINTED IN THE UNITED STATES OF AMERICA
ON ACID-FREE PAPER
BY HADDON CRAFTSMEN, BLOOMSBURG, PENNSYLVANIA

In loving memory of my grandmother

A'ida Radel Rosenthal

who told me wonderful stories of her childhood
in Argentina and New York City.

I want to thank the many people who helped me brush up on my Spanish:

Nellie Colledanchise, Solange and Guillermo DiGenova,
Barbara Ferrer, Nancy and Johnny Matias,
Francisco and Solangel Parra, Francesca Robbins,
Jorgé Rodriguez, Maurice Roque,
Caridad Piñeiro Scordato, and Manoli Wenz.

Thank you to Henry Acevedo and family for letting me "borrow" their last name. Muchas gracias, mis amigos!

And a BIG thank you to my cousin Dr. Michele Rosenthal for help with the emergency room scenes!

Chapter One

"Your grandmother was injured doing the salsa?"

Marisol Acevedo felt herself flush as the emergency room nurse stared at her in obvious disbelief. Even to her own ears it sounded kind of crazy. A seventy-year-old grandmother attempting to learn the salsa? And being stepped on by a seventeen-year-old grandson?

"Yes," she began, but her cousin José interrupted.

"It was my fault. I wasn't being careful enough and I stepped on her foot." He shot their grandma a contrite look.

"It's not your fault," Grandma Margarita said staunchly as she sat on the emergency room bed.

"We think her toe might be broken," Marisol told the nurse. "I was trying to teach her to salsa—"

"For Yolanda's wedding," Grandma rushed on.

"Uh . . . well . . ." The nurse made a note on the paper

1

attached to her clipboard. "Dr. Lares will be here in a moment to see you." She escaped from the small examining room as if she was anxious to get away from these *loco* people.

Marisol sent her cousin and grandmother a grin. "She thinks we're crazy. It does sound kind of funny, doesn't it?" She could just see the headlines: *70-Year-Old Grandmother Injured While Performing Salsa Moves.*

Something was nagging at her memory, though. Something about the doctor's name—where had she heard it before? She thought about it, breathing in the medicinal smell of the hospital.

"Dr. Lares," murmured Grandma, "a nice name . . ."

"Dr. Alejandro Lares?" Hearing the surprise in her cousin's voice, Marisol pivoted to look at him. He snapped his cell phone shut and came forward. "I still can't reach your mother and father," he said. "Or mine."

Marisol sighed. "They must have turned off their cell phones again. Mama doesn't like it when they're visiting friends and the phone is always ringing. And Papa usually forgets his anyway." Curious, she went back to her cousin's question. "Do you know the doctor?"

"*Everyone's* heard of Alejandro Lares," José stated with typical teenage assurance. "They still talk about him at school, even though he graduated a long time ago."

Then the name clicked in, and Marisol remembered why it sounded so familiar. "Not that long ago," she said dryly. "Maybe five or six years before me? And yes, I heard stories about him too." About the kid who read the encyclopedia for fun, when he'd finished his work way ahead of his classmates. About Alejandro being the first Hispanic student from their high school to be class valedictorian . . . and the only one to go to an Ivy League school. About his scholarships, his success on the soccer team, his getting into a good medical school . . . the list went on and on.

She hadn't known he'd come back to the Dover area once he'd become a physician.

"He was on the soccer team—" Marisol began, knowing how much her cousin loved soccer, when the curtain to the examining room was pushed aside and in walked the doctor.

The tag proclaimed him to be Dr. Alex Lares.

He might not be the standard "tall," but the expression "dark and handsome" certainly fit. Dr. Lares was medium height, with thick, night-black hair and a classically handsome face. Straight nose, nice cheekbones, eyes that were a deep brown. His dark skin was smooth, and his handsome features wore an expression that was all business.

"Mrs. Soto?" he asked, moving over to Grandma.

Marisol realized with a start that she must have been staring at him. She quickly moved closer to her grandmother, turning to regard her.

Her grandmother was staring at him too.

After a glance at the chart in his hand, he said, "Tell me what happened," in a soothing tone.

Grandma began in English, "I was learning the salsa with my grandson José, and it was my fault, I got in the way—"

The doctor's eyebrows shot up.

"No, *Mamita,*" José interrupted, calling her by the affectionate term they used. "It was my fault, I stepped on your toe—"

"No, no, it was my fault—" Grandma overrode his voice. "And it hurts a little—"

"—a lot—" José said.

"We think her toe may be broken," Marisol finished.

Dr. Lares turned and looked at her.

Their eyes met, and she felt a spark race down to her toes.

Then he turned back to her grandma. His tone was kind as he said, "Tell me if this hurts."

He prodded her toe, and Grandma's wincing was proof enough.

"It is not so very bad," she added hastily, in Spanish.

"It may be broken, or perhaps it is a bad sprain," he told her in Spanish too, his accent different than theirs and his wording more formal. He turned to look at Marisol again. "We will need to take an X-ray."

Marisol nodded, concern for her grandmother overriding the instant attraction she felt toward the handsome doctor. What a time to be feeling something like this!

"I'll have someone here to take you to X-ray in a few minutes," he told *Mamita.* "Fortunately, we are not busy tonight, so we'll get you right in."

He disappeared, and Marisol stared at the spot where he'd stood moments ago.

Dr. Alejandro Lares was incredibly good-looking.

But she shouldn't be thinking that now!

"He is handsome, *sí*?" Grandma said in Spanish, echoing Marisol's thoughts.

"*Sí*," she replied automatically, then turned to look at her grandmother. "*Mamita—*"

"And not married either," her grandmother said, winking. "I checked. He wore no wedding ring."

"That doesn't always mean—" Marisol stopped. She didn't want her grandmother getting any ideas. After tonight, the good-looking doctor would be out of their lives. Did it matter that she felt a compelling attraction to the man?

Moments later, an assistant parted the curtains, and with a smile, he told them he was here to take Grandma to get her X-ray.

While they waited, José went to the lobby to try Marisol's parents on his cell phone again, hoping to get better reception. And Marisol was left to worry about her grandmother and to try to push away any romantic thoughts of the handsome doctor.

She glanced at her watch. Her young cousin Christina should be home from her friend's house across the street any minute. She could call Christina and ask her to try and track down her parents. Christina was living with them for the rest of the school year and the next. Her dad had taken a job down in Florida and she wanted to stay up in New Jersey to finish school, so it had been decided that she would stay at Marisol's family's home.

Or maybe José would get hold of his parents, who lived around the corner from Marisol's, if he couldn't reach her mom and dad.

Marisol noticed she wasn't getting reception in this room, and decided to tell José to call Christina when he returned. In the meantime she didn't want to leave the room because she was hoping Grandma would come back soon.

She was surprised and pleased when her grandmother was wheeled in a few minutes later, her face still looking calm, although Marisol knew she was in pain.

José returned. "I just got hold of them. They're on their way over."

Relief rushed through her. She might be twenty-six years old, but it was still nice to have parents to lean on.

The curtains parted and Dr. Lares came in again.

"I have good news," he said in a cheerful voice. "*Señora*, you have a bad sprain, but your toe is not broken."

Marisol felt another heady wave of relief.

"Just a sprain?" she asked, wanting to make sure she had heard right.

"Yes." The handsome doctor turned toward her. "But a sprain can sometimes be even more painful than a broken bone. I'm going to give your grandmother some painkillers, for her to take when she needs them." He turned back toward Grandma Margarita. "These could make you sleepy, so don't drive if you're taking them, or do too much. Or," he added dryly, with a glance at Marisol and José, "don't attempt the salsa while under the influence of these pills."

Grandma grinned. "I won't, doctor."

Marisol found herself smiling too. "We'll make sure

she doesn't, but I'm afraid it was my fault. I was trying to teach her so she could salsa at cousin Yolanda's wedding—"

"No, it's not your fault, I asked for a lesson," Grandma interrupted. "Everyone's learning for the wedding." She shot the doctor a glance that Marisol thought looked almost flirtatious. "My granddaughter Marisol"—she indicated her—"is one of the teachers at Bailemos! And she agreed to help me."

"Assistant teacher," Marisol corrected her hastily. "I just help with an introductory class," she told Dr. Lares.

The doctor raised his eyebrows. "That's funny," he said. "I signed up for a Tuesday class at Bailemos! that starts next week."

Marisol felt her pulse speed up.

"My cousin Pablo is getting married in August and I'm the best man. He insisted I needed to take this class with him and his fiancé so I could dance at their wedding," Dr. Lares finished.

Marisol couldn't help the spurt of excitement that was shooting through her. Dr. Lares would be in the class that she helped teach!

Grandma was practically beaming now. "Tuesday is when Marisol teaches," she told the doctor.

"It is?" He turned to regard her again. Marisol wished she could decipher his expression. He seemed surprised—and possibly, she thought, glad? Or was that her overly active imagination?

"I'm only an assistant teacher," she said hastily. "My real job is as a children's librarian."

"Ahh." She wondered what that meant. He turned to Grandma. "Of course, I never realized the salsa was so dangerous," he continued.

"Oh, no, it's not—" Marisol began, then saw his smile. He was teasing.

Dr. Alex Lares' smile was unexpected and transformed his face from simply handsome to gorgeous.

Marisol found herself smiling back. "I'll see you in class next week, and I promise to make it as safe as possible," she told him.

"I'll count on that. Now," he said, returning to his serious expression, "let me give you some instructions for your grandmother—she lives with you, correct?"

At Marisol's nod, he went on to tell her about a special shoe a nurse would bring in, and to give some general directions for Grandma. "And she should go see her own doctor in a few days, so he can determine how she is healing," he finished. "Any questions?"

They had none. Marisol noticed that both Grandma and José had been studying the doctor as he spoke.

"Then I hope you feel better, *señora*," he began, when a nurse pulled the curtain back.

"Doctor, a possible heart attack patient just arrived," she said.

"I'm coming." He smiled at them all. "Take care." He moved swiftly out of the room.

As soon as he left, Grandma gave a wide smile. "You're going to see him again, *niña*!"

A sudden commotion and her mother's anxious voice sounded from the hall before Marisol could answer.

"Here's your mom and dad," José said.

Marisol was glad for the distraction. She didn't want anyone—especially her sharp grandmother—seeing how happy she was at the knowledge that she'd see Dr. Alex Lares again so soon.

She hadn't felt so attracted to a man in a long time. A really long time.

She couldn't wait to see him again.

Alex sighed and rubbed his neck. His shift would end soon. Thursday nights were generally not too bad, and this was no exception. A boy who broke his arm skateboarding, a man with an asthma attack—the weather had been more warm and humid than usual for late May in northern New Jersey—and the eighty-two-year-old man who had had a heart attack were among his patients for the evening. It had been touch and go with the heart attack case, but they'd pulled him through, and he was now on his way up to intensive care.

And, of course, Margarita Soto, the dancing grandmother who'd sprained her toe and come in with her family.

He'd managed to push aside thoughts of her beautiful granddaughter while he concentrated on his patients. When there was an emergency to care for, he got right to work and did what he had to do. There was simply no time for thoughts about anything else.

Now that the evening's emergencies were over and his notes were made, he was free to think back on the evening. And the people he'd treated, and seen.

Margarita Soto's granddaughter stood out from all the others.

She was gorgeous. There was simply no other word for it. Petite, with curly black hair that spilled over her shoulders, hazel brown eyes that sparkled, and a wide, cheerful smile—she was the kind of woman you didn't forget. She'd worn a red T-shirt and khaki skirt, and her figure was slim but curvy. Her voice was melodious and wonderfully pleasing. No, you wouldn't forget her easily. In fact, most men would be drooling after meeting the beautiful salsa teacher.

Most men . . . including Alejandro Lares.

He rubbed his eyes, beginning to feel weary. Was Marisol attracted to him? He wondered, rather grimly, if he'd ever find a woman who was interested in him, the real Alejandro, his personality, his likes and dislikes. Juanita certainly hadn't been—

"Doctor?" Nurse Davis was rapidly approaching. "They're bringing in a victim from a car accident on Route 80. Possible broken bones."

Alex sighed. Work wasn't over yet.

Marisol found herself scanning the group of new students in the introductory salsa class.

She couldn't help it. Alejandro Lares had invaded her thoughts often since Thursday night, when her grandmother was injured.

Luckily *Mamita* was doing better, getting around almost as well as usual, and after the first two days, she'd been uncomfortable but not in bad pain.

As Sondra, the head teacher, began to speak about the basics of salsa, Marisol listened with half an ear. She knew this part well. Sondra always went over a little bit about the history of salsa or some interesting information at the start of each night of the class.

"We believe the roots of salsa come from folk dances in Cuba and Puerto Rico," Sondra was saying, "and have been influenced by the music of the 'big band' era . . ."

There was a good-size group this time, Marisol observed. Over twenty people, although she didn't see Alex yet. Her heart dropped. Wasn't he coming?

"Oh, look at these guys coming in," whispered Celia, the other assistant teacher, from behind Marisol. "Ohh . . . they are handsome."

Marisol looked toward the door. Entering the room were Alejandro Lares and another man.

Alex, in khakis and a dark shirt, looked even better than she remembered. Her heart skipped. He seemed to be looking over the group for something.

Or someone? Maybe her?

The other man appeared to be about Alex's age and was also good-looking. They were almost the same height, with Alex being slightly taller, and she thought there was a definite resemblance. This must be his cousin.

A woman with short brown hair moved over to greet them. Marisol guessed that she was the cousin's fiancé. She knew she was right when the man with Alex leaned down to give her a quick kiss.

"Come join us," Sondra commanded. Then she continued with her speech. "Deejays on the West Coast were probably the first to call this music salsa music . . ."

Marisol tried not to stare and focused on Sondra.

Marisol and Celia were both assistants because they'd been taking classes for over a year. Marisol loved dancing, especially the salsa. Not only was it fun, but the movements were graceful. Of course, timing and precision were important too, but she didn't mind practicing. She wasn't sure she wanted to do the competitions some of the advanced students got into, but she didn't mind doing demonstrations and being an assistant teacher. It was a nice contrast to her work as a librarian. Since they often had more female students than males, she had been taught to take the male's part too, so she could fill in when necessary.

Celia, like Marisol, was only a part-time teacher, and had another job as an office manager at an insurance company in town.

"Here comes one more late student," Celia whispered. "That makes twenty-four—that should be everyone."

Marisol glanced over to the door, then froze.

Leo was walking into the room.

Leo was taking this class?

Leo Sanchez was a guy she'd known for over a year. Known, and liked, in a casual way. They'd become friendly when she started working at the library in a nearby town. He'd come in to do some research on a day when the reference librarian was out sick. He was an accountant taking some college classes for his master's degree, and because he didn't have the time to go to the college library, but needed help to research, he'd come to Marisol's library. Marisol had assisted him, and he'd asked her out. She thought he was nice, but there'd been no spark. After a few dates she'd suggested that they just be friends, and he seemed fine with that. They saw each other occasionally, and despite the fact that her family was always asking if they were going out together, she knew she just didn't feel that way about Leo.

But about a month ago, she'd gotten the feeling that he wanted to change all that. She'd responded by spending less time with him, feeling uncomfortable about the whole thing.

Now he was in her salsa class?

She wanted to groan. Just when she had an opportunity to know Alex better!

Although, she had to admit, with fourteen women and only ten men in the class, she and Celia would not have much chance to mingle with the guys. They'd probably be dancing the part of the males most of the time.

Well, at least during the break she would get a chance to say hello to Alex.

If Leo didn't corner her first.

No, she decided, she was not going to let that happen.

Leo was staring at her. She gave him a smile, smaller than her normal smile, and then turned her attention back to Sondra.

"The beat is, one-two-three pause, five-six-seven pause," Sondra instructed.

Sondra had everyone line up. She introduced Marisol and Celia, and they went to the front of the room, on either side. Sondra then began demonstrating the basic steps, with Marsiol and Celia in sync with her motions, so no matter where the students stood, they could see one of the three.

After the students had tried the steps several times, Sondra took the male part and had Marisol dance a few steps with her so the students could see how a couple moved. Then, she had them practice again. Finally, she divided the class up into partners.

Marisol had moved away from Leo, afraid he would try to claim her as a dance partner. He had never before seemed to have any interest in learning to salsa, and she suspected his showing up here had more to do with his attempts to get closer to her these last few weeks than in any real interest in dancing.

Marisol found herself partnered with a short, middle-aged plump woman with blond hair and big glasses.

"I'm Stella Dowd," the woman introduced herself enthusiastically. "I couldn't persuade my husband to take this class, so I told him, Jack, I'm going by myself! And here I am," she finished proudly.

"I'm sure you'll enjoy it," Marisol responded, "and after he sees how much fun you're having, maybe he'll want to try it too. That happens often, actually."

Stella sniffed. "Hmph. That's if I want him to come with me."

They began to practice the steps without the music. Marisol helped guide Stella, who seemed to be catching on quickly. She looked up and glanced around, wondering who Alex was paired with.

He was dancing with a tall, attractive brunette.

Marisol had to resist gritting her teeth.

She noticed that Leo had been paired with a woman who must have been around sixty. It served him right, she thought, trying not to smile too much. He should have told her he was signing up for the class.

Sondra put on a CD, and they tried the basic steps a dozen times while the hot Latin music filled the room.

Then she called for a switch in partners. This time Marisol was paired with a man of about forty who had come with his wife, who was now dancing with Stella. Marisol had to avoid the man's feet as he seemed to be having trouble following the steps.

"Here, let's take it slow," she said, and helped him in slow motion to follow the correct steps.

After a few minutes of coaching, her partner seemed to catch on. When she had a chance, she glanced around the room. This time, Alex was dancing with his cousin's fiancé. And Celia had ended up with his cousin.

Alex turned slightly, and his eyes met Marisol's.

Something sparked between them. She was sure of it.

But then her partner bumped into her, and almost trod on her foot. Hastily, she brought her attention back to him, and patiently helped guide him back to the correct movements.

Just as he seemed to be getting accustomed to the steps, Sondra called a fifteen-minute break.

The students gravitated toward a table in the lobby

that held cold water, lemonade, and hot water for coffee or tea. The cold water and lemonade appeared to be the favorites tonight. Marisol had her own water bottle, and went to retrieve it, then moved toward the lobby, slowly searching for the man who had been on her mind so much lately.

She found Alex talking to the couple she believed was his cousin and his cousin's fiancé. As she approached, his eyes met hers and he smiled, once again transforming his serious expression to a lighter one.

She smiled back. "Dr. Lares," she murmured as she drew close. "I hope you're enjoying the class?"

"Please call me Alex. I am enjoying the class," he answered emphatically, regarding her. "I didn't think I would"—he paused and shot the man who looked like him a glance—"but I am. And so far," he added, "it hasn't been very dangerous."

"I told you," Marisol said with a laugh, "we'd try to keep you safe!"

"And how is your grandmother?" he asked.

"Very well, thank you. She's feeling much better."

"Introduce us, Alex," the other man said.

"Oh, Marisol, this is my cousin, Pablo Lares," Alex said hastily. "And his fiancé, Irena Santos. This is Marisol Acevedo," he told them.

He'd obviously remembered her name from Sondra's brief introduction during class. Marisol couldn't help but be pleased as she greeted his cousin and the young woman with him. Like Alex, Pablo had very dark hair and eyes, although he was shorter and perhaps a couple of years younger. Irena had short brown hair and a big smile.

Marisol asked them about their wedding plans, and Irena mentioned they were getting married in August.

"We want to be able to salsa at the wedding!" Irena declared.

"You'll know it by then!" Marisol was saying, when she felt someone sidle up to her.

She turned slightly to find Leo there, grinning rather sheepishly.

"Hello, Marisol," he said.

She tried to curb the annoyance that spurted through her.

"Hello," she replied, keeping her voice deliberately neutral. What she really wanted was to jab him and say, "What are you doing here?"

Instead, she turned to the others. "This is Leo Sanchez—a *friend* of mine." She placed special emphasis on the word *friend*. "He's taking the class for the first time, right, Leo?" She pasted a stiff smile on her face as she turned back to him.

"Yes, I decided to sign up just last week," he said hastily.

And somehow conveniently forgot to tell me, Marisol thought.

She introduced Irena, Pablo, and Alex, and noticed Irena was staring at Leo.

"Didn't I see you at the North Jersey Accountants' Dinner a couple of weeks ago?" she asked him.

"You were there?" He sounded surprised. "Yes, I was

there too. I work for Jackson, Castellano and Levine . . . who do you work for?"

As Irena started to reply, Marisol edged away from Leo. Sondra liked the teachers to circulate among the students during break time. Although Marisol was reluctant to move away from Alex, she had no desire to encourage Leo.

"I have to circulate," she apologized to Alex. "Maybe we'll have a chance to talk later."

"I'd like that," he said simply.

Marisol moved on to Stella and another woman who was talking to her. Then she stopped to speak to a young couple who, like Alex's cousin, were engaged and wanted to learn to salsa before their wedding.

When Sondra called the class together again Marisol noticed that Leo was still with Alex, Irena, and Pablo. She frowned, hoping Leo wasn't suggesting that she was actually dating him. She'd have to set Alex straight if that was what Leo was doing.

After she gave it to Leo, of course.

Maybe she shouldn't be so suspicious. Maybe Leo was simply talking to them because he didn't know anyone else in the class.

This time, Marisol was paired up with a woman of about thirty who revealed she'd wanted to learn the salsa for years. Sondra had them repeat the basic steps they'd already learned, and then Marisol and Celia went to the front of the class to demonstrate again. This time they added swaying hips to the basic steps.

Before Marisol knew it, the class was having their

second break. She noticed Celia had gravitated to Alex and his group. Knowing they should speak to different people, she went over to a group of young adults and spoke to them for a while.

Leo, she noticed, was hanging around the edges of the class.

She pointedly ignored him, still annoyed.

After speaking to her group, she went to get some lemonade, and Celia joined her.

"That handsome doctor over there was asking about you," she said in a hushed voice. "Isn't he good-looking? And his cousin too!" She shot them a dreamy glance.

"Yes," Marisol agreed, but didn't reveal she'd met Alex before. "His cousin's engaged, you know."

"I know. All the good ones get taken fast," Celia said with a sigh. "Here I am, twenty-seven, with no boyfriend in sight." Celia, an attractive woman with long, straight, light brown hair, had broken up a year ago with a guy who drank too much. She had enjoyed playing the field for a while. But now Marisol thought she might want to settle down. "My family is on my back about getting married."

"Mine gets like that too," Marisol admitted. Her grandmother had been a mere seventeen when she married in Puerto Rico. Her parents had both grown up in Dover, and her mother had been twenty, and her father twenty-two when they married. They had expected that she and her brother and sister would follow their pattern of marrying young. Marisol's brother, who was the oldest, had waited till he was twenty-five to get married. But her sister had been twenty-three when she married five years ago. Now here she, Marisol, was, twenty-six, and still single. She knew her parents were worried. She did want to get married—but she wanted to marry the right guy. And so far he hadn't appeared.

Without volition, she looked at Alex.

As if he sensed her glance, he turned and his eyes met hers.

Sharp clapping startled Marisol, interrupting the moment. Sondra was announcing the end of the break.

The rest of the class sped by. Although the first couple of classes were more difficult, with students learning the basics and making many mistakes, Marisol loved dancing and teaching the salsa. It was fun and with the hot, bright music, it didn't seem like work. The clicks of shoes against polished wood were both familiar and invigorating.

At the end of the lesson Sondra praised everyone for catching on quickly and promised some new variations for next week.

"And in a few weeks my husband will join us and we'll demonstrate some advanced moves," she told the class. "Right now he's in Mexico on a business trip."

She, Marisol, and Celia circulated and said good-bye to the students as they left. The room was warm, but everyone seemed reluctant to leave.

"This class *really* seems to be enjoying dancing," Sondra said to Marisol. Then she went to say good-bye to a particularly enthusiastic couple.

Marisol expected Leo to hang around and talk to her,

and she saw him near the door, waiting. Several people said something to him as they left. It seemed that even the straight-laced Leo had enjoyed the class.

She glanced around the room, looking for Alex, and found him talking to his cousin Pablo, Irena, and Celia.

She went over to the group.

"Marisol!" Irena exclaimed. "We were just saying that we should get a group together and go out after class for a drink or a snack or something."

"That sounds like a good idea," Marisol answered.

"I'd love to," Celia added. "I'm always hungry and thirsty after class!"

Alex regarded her. "I have an early morning tomorrow," he said. "But maybe next week?"

"Yes, next week would be good," Irena continued. Looking beyond Marisol, she finished, "and Leo, why don't you join us? And we can ask Dominick and Anne—" She indicated the engaged couple who stood nearby.

Marisol looked straight at Alex and couldn't help the smile that she felt spreading over her face. "I'd like that. Next Tuesday, then!"

"See you then," he said as Irena called the other young couple over.

Gradually the rest of the class left and Marisol was relieved that Leo went out with the other students. She and Celia helped Sondra straighten up and then lock up the school, which was headquartered in a former store on Blackwell Street. At nine thirty at night the street was quiet but well lit, but they all left together, always safety-conscious in the little city that was Marisol's home. When her mother had been growing up this had been a rougher town, and though a lot of the town had been "cleaned up" and made safer, none of them wanted to take chances. They walked together to the parking lot just a few doors down.

Marisol was still annoyed with Leo, but relieved to see he hadn't waited for her. Good. She didn't want Leo—or anyone else—thinking he had a claim on her. She was not dating Leo.

Right now, there was only one man who piqued her interest.

Alejandro Lares.

Chapter Two

"So tomorrow you get to see Alex, right?"

Marisol's young cousin Christina—or Christa as she preferred to be called—perched on the bed where Marisol was sitting, trying to decide whether to start a Harry Potter book she hadn't read yet, or the new thriller by a best-selling author. Marisol glanced up at her.

"Yes . . . ," she murmured. She'd admitted to Christa that she had been thinking about the handsome doctor quite a bit. Christa had been fascinated by the whole story of their meeting and then his attending the salsa class.

"So what are you wearing?" Christa asked with great interest.

Marisol had to smile. Her cousin was a typical seventeen-year-old—sweet, smart, and concerned with fashion.

Christa had been very upset when her father took a job in Florida a few months ago. She'd dreaded leaving her friends and the neighborhood she'd grown up in, especially since she was at the end of her junior year of high school. With only a little over a year left, Marisol's parents had invited her to stay with them. Their cozy Cape Cod–style home had room—Marisol's brother, Pedro Junior, was married and had two children; and her sister, Anita, had gotten married several years ago, and had one child and another on the way. With more room in the house, Grandma had moved into Junior's old room when Grandpa died five years ago, and Christa had recently moved into the large upstairs room Marisol used to share with her sister.

"I was thinking of wearing my light blue dress," Marisol said. "Or maybe the dark green sleeveless top with the black skirt—"

"Wear the blue dress," Christa advised. "You look gorgeous in it."

Marisol smiled. "Thanks. So what's doing with you and Matt?" Matt was Christa's boyfriend—this week, anyway.

"Oh, I don't know. I think we're going our separate ways," she said, sounding as wise as an owl. She didn't sound particularly upset about it either. Marisol suppressed a smile. She was twenty-six, but could easily remember how vital everything seemed when you were seventeen, and how smart teens thought they were.

A warm breeze blew in the open window. It was a

nice evening in early June, not quite hot enough for air-conditioning like it had been the last week in May. Maybe she'd suggest a walk with Christa.

She opened her mouth to, when they heard the door-bell, followed by barking.

"I'll answer it," Christa announced, and zipped down-stairs.

Marisol hoped it wasn't Leo again.

He'd called the day after the salsa class and asked if she wanted to go out on Friday. She had coolly replied that she was busy.

"Leo, what made you sign up for the salsa class?" she had asked.

"Oh, nothing . . . I just thought I'd try it," he'd said airily.

She couldn't quite believe that. On Saturday after-noon, she'd been working, but her mother had reported that he'd dropped by her house. Not that he hadn't done that in the past but—she was certain he was trying to get more romantic with her. She'd definitely have to put a stop to it, she decided.

She heard voices, and went to see who was down-stairs. If it was Leo, she might as well get the conversa-tion over with.

But it wasn't. It was Manuel, an elderly widower who lived next door with his daughter and son-in-law. He had moved in just a few months ago, and occasionally he and Grandma watched TV together or went for a walk with his dog, Priscilla, and Pepé, the Acevedos' dog.

Manuel greeted Marisol and asked if she wanted to watch a funny show on a Spanish channel with him and Grandma.

"No, you two go ahead," Marisol said.

Her parents were visiting her Aunt Sophie and her family just two blocks away, so Marisol and Christa left Margarita and Manuel to enjoy the show with the two dogs sitting at their feet.

It was kind of cute, Marisol thought as she returned to her room, that *Mamita* seemed to have a gentleman friend!

Christa followed her upstairs, now on her cell phone with a friend. "And he said to her, 'What do you mean you don't want to go out with me?' like he couldn't believe it . . ."

Marisol tried to tune out the conversation and settle down with the thriller novel. But thoughts of Alejandro Lares kept intruding.

She couldn't wait to see him again!

Alex entered the dance studio at seven twenty, ten minutes early. He'd come with Pablo last week, at Pablo's insistence, but Pablo had been running late.

He didn't want to be late again, so he'd decided to arrive on his own.

There were a number of students already milling around in the lobby. He heard music and feet tap-tap-tapping from the class that ran before theirs. He looked over the crowd, wondering if he'd see Marisol.

She must be in the studio room or in an office, because

he didn't see her in the lobby. He did, however, see that guy, Leo, who had been hanging around her with an expression Alex didn't care for. An expression of . . . well . . . like he had a thing for her. He figured the guy was attracted to Marisol, despite the fact that she'd called him a friend.

The doors at the back of the lobby opened and a bunch of young girls walked out, giggling and talking, and were met by some mothers who sat in a corner.

The people from the salsa class began to move forward.

"This is going to be such fun!" Irena said from behind Alex.

Alex turned. He hadn't noticed Pablo and Irena come in. He'd been too busy searching for the lovely Miss Acevedo.

He spotted her then, in a corner with the head teacher, Sondra, and his mouth went dry.

She looked gorgeous.

Marisol was dressed in a light blue dress with a wide skirt that showed off her slim but curvy figure and her tanned legs. Her curly dark hair swept her shoulders, and gold hoop earrings peeked through the strands of her hair. His fingers flexed, as if they wanted to run through her silky locks.

She was smiling at an older couple, her smile wide and genuine, and part of him yearned to have her turn that melting, happy smile on him.

She moved her head slightly, and her gaze met his.

And now that dazzling smile *was* focused on him. He

smiled back, and he thought—he hoped—he caught an answering flash in her eyes.

Was it possible she was attracted to him too?

He'd had plenty of women smile invitingly at him before . . . but somehow Marisol's smile was special. He wanted to feel its warmth on him. Often.

Sondra, the head teacher, was clapping her hands and directing people to form lines. Within minutes, they were reviewing the basic steps from last week, and Alex had to concentrate. Dancing might come naturally for some, like Pablo, but he had to work at it. He was finding it especially difficult to have his hips moving in the opposite direction from the way his foot moved.

Maybe Marisol could help him. He hoped he would have a chance to dance with the beautiful teacher tonight.

But if he didn't, there was still this after-class social that Irena had organized. Hopefully, Marisol still intended to join the others for a bite to eat.

He tried to concentrate on the dance as Sondra taught them a new variation.

When they were partnered, he ended up with a gregarious woman who he thought was about his age. She talked so much he was having trouble following the music. He looked around, rather desperately, wondering if he could somehow get close to Marisol so she would be his next partner.

Marisol noticed Alex looking around as he strove to follow the steps of the dance, which were becoming increasingly complicated. The woman with him appeared to be chatting incessantly, and she made a mental note to ask Sondra to speak to her quietly. For many students, it was hard to concentrate on the steps with any distractions.

Sondra called a change of partners and they moved three people to the right. Marisol faced Leo.

"Hi!" he said, his smile a beatific one. He seemed to have doused himself with his favorite cologne, and Marisol had to stop herself from wrinkling her nose from the strength of it.

"Hello." She kept her voice cool. As they began to dance, he pulled her a little too close. She responded by pulling back a little too far.

She repeated her question from their phone conversation last week. "Leo," she whispered, "why are you taking this class?" His statement that he just felt like trying it had been hard to believe.

This time he responded swiftly. "To be with you."

Well. That answered *that* question. It was just what she'd feared. She might as well tackle this subject now. "Leo, we agreed to be friends," she hissed. "Remember?"

"I remember." He gave her a rather smug look. "But that was last year. What if I've changed my mind?"

"I haven't changed mine," she shot back.

He stumbled, then retrieved his balance.

"Maybe you will." He smiled winningly. Marisol suspected that Leo couldn't imagine that he wasn't her ideal boyfriend. He'd always had a slight superiority about him. At first she'd thought he was simply proud to be an accountant. Like her, he was the first in his Puerto Rican family to go to college and become a professional. But maybe his attitude was just a form of simple conceit. He was an only child, and his parents doted on him.

She managed to shake her head as they followed the salsa's steps. "No, I won't."

"I can be very persuasive," Leo said.

"No," she repeated. Taking pity on his suddenly disappointed expression, she added, "We're good friends, Leo. Let's leave it at that. Some other woman out there will appreciate all your fine qualities . . ."

He trod on her foot.

"Oops! Sorry," he said hastily. "Look, let's see what happens, okay? I can be just what you want in a boyfriend."

Marisol shook her head.

"We're still going for a snack after class, right?" he asked. Now he sounded slightly anxious.

Marisol sighed. She was tempted to say no, but she really did want to go. Irena had indicated before class started that she had organized a whole group to go— her fiancé and Alex, Marisol and Celia, Leo and the engaged couple Anne and Dominick, plus another single woman named Shannon and a man in his early thirties named Xavier.

Marisol really wanted to go.

"Yes, I'm going," she said. "But I'd really rather not discuss this situation there."

Leo smiled, as if he thought this was a good thing, and Marisol sighed again, to herself, as Sondra called for a break.

The rest of the class flew by. Marisol didn't get to dance with Alex, but she did dance with Pablo, who seemed to be a nice guy. He was a little more outgoing than Alex, though not nearly as talkative as his fiancé, Irena. From Pablo she learned that his parents and Alex's had come from Argentina at the same time, and settled in Dover near each other. Their fathers were brothers.

After class, they gathered in the lobby. Marisol and Celia had to straighten up, and agreed to meet the others in a few minutes at the Mexican restaurant that was half a mile away.

"We can get appetizers," Irena said. "We'll save you seats."

Marisol and Celia worked faster than usual, and Marisol wondered if Celia was eager to spend time with anyone particular in the group. Not Alex, she hoped. Maybe she could try to get Celia together with Leo?

Now that was an appealing idea, although she suspected Leo might be too conservative for the rather flamboyant Celia.

Celia, with her pretty face, long straight hair, and very curvy body, attracted a lot of men. But most of them were the wrong types. She had confided to Marisol on more than one occasion that she could never seem to find a guy who was stable. The men she dated—mostly handsome guys to whom she was attracted—seemed to be immature, or had trouble holding on to a job, or, like her last boyfriend, drank too much.

She really needed someone nice and steady and

responsible, Marisol mused, and determined to try to get Celia close to Leo.

They found spaces in the restaurant's parking lot and walked in together. On a Tuesday it wasn't overly crowded. The group from the dance studio had pushed several tables together, and as Marisol and Celia approached, a waiter was placing two appetizer sampler trays on the table.

"We got the samplers," Irena greeted them, indicating two empty seats on opposite sides. "If you want something else, he'll take your orders."

Celia ordered a strawberry margarita and a cheeseburger, while Marisol decided to stick to the appetizers and a Diet Coke. She slid into the seat that was between Alex and Leo, hoping it was Alex and not Leo who had saved the space. Leo was actually talking to Irena, and she heard the phrase "tax exemptions" before she turned to look at Alex.

"Hi," he said softly, regarding her.

She saw Celia scoot in between Pablo and Xavier, then turned her full attention to Alex.

"Are you enjoying the class?" she asked.

The room was dark and atmospheric, but she thought she could see a gleam in his eyes. "Very much so. More than I thought I would," he told her. After a hesitation, he added, "I think the teachers are wonderful. Especially you," he added, his tone dropping low.

A tingle shot up Marisol's spine.

"I'm so glad," she responded. "Maybe you'll sign up to take the advanced class?"

But he shook his head. "Dancing isn't really my thing," he said. "I'll be lucky to get through the beginners' course."

Disappointment plunged through her, erasing the thrill she'd felt a moment before.

"Well, think about it," she urged. "There are only six more sessions left in the beginners' class."

"Here, Marisol." Leo was passing the platter of mixed appetizers. Marisol picked up a small quesadilla and took a bite. She savored the spicy taste, wondering all the while how she could convince Alex to take another set of classes.

And how on earth was she going to get Celia to speak to Leo? A glance showed her that Celia was animatedly talking to Xavier and Pablo.

Latin music was playing in the background. An idea began to form. If she could get Celia to dance with Leo . . .

And why not try to get Alex to dance with you? a little voice inside her asked.

"How did you do with the new steps we learned today?" Marisol asked Alex.

"Those new steps today were difficult," Irena declared before Alex could reply, then she dipped a chip in guacamole. "I was having trouble concentrating . . ."

The song that was playing ended, and almost immediately, a hot salsa tune began.

This was her chance.

She gave Alex a big smile, and extended her hand.

"Come salsa with me," she invited.

She observed Alex's look of surprise, and stiff posture. Obviously, he was hesitant. She smiled at him and said softly, "C'mon, let's dance."

She could see the battle waging in his head. Was he afraid to dance alone with her in front of his cousin? Or was it a general unease about doing the salsa in public?

He opened his mouth, and she thought he was going to say no.

But then Irena got up, and pulled Pablo to his feet. And Anne and Dominick followed.

Alex glanced at them, then back at Marisol. "All right," he said.

He stood and took her hand. Her hand felt warm and cozy in his, and she didn't care if everyone was staring at them. This felt so right.

Once beside Anne and Dominick, Alex assumed his position. Her heartbeat increased as she placed one hand on his shoulder and slipped her other hand into his. She had dreamed about dancing with Alex like this, and now it was really happening. She was determined to enjoy every second.

The restaurant was dark, and although smoking wasn't allowed, the atmosphere was thick and intimate. She could smell the tantalizing food and hear the clink of glasses and voices in the background. The Latin music seemed to surround them like a warm cloud.

She smelled Alex's spicy aftershave, and with her head so close to his, she could see the beginnings of dark, bearded shadows on his face.

His eyes met hers, and a jolt of pure electricity zapped her.

Dancing with him like this was heavenly.

His steps were hesitant, so she found herself guiding him a little as they swayed to the music, doing the basic steps again and again. As they turned, she saw Leo looking at them, frowning. She didn't care. This was where she wanted to be. In fact, if she could, she would stay like this for the next few hours.

"You dance so well," Alex whispered, his breath warm against her cheek.

"Thank you. You're doing great for someone who's just had two lessons," she praised him. He *was* doing fine for a beginner.

He smiled. "Not really."

"Yes," she insisted. "*Es verdad,*" she said, slipping into Spanish for "it's true." "Lots of beginners aren't as smooth," she finished.

He raised his eyebrows.

She wondered how someone as brilliant as Alex could have any doubts about his abilities. Brilliant and handsome, she thought. Was it her imagination or was he gripping her hand tighter as he gazed into her eyes?

Marisol wanted to melt further into his arms.

But the music was ending . . . too soon, she thought with regret.

"That was fun," she whispered.

He regarded her. "Yes, it was. Would you—would you consider giving me a private lesson?"

Her surprise must have shown on her face.

"A private lesson?" she asked. Usually Sondra was the one to do those. But oh, the idea was tempting . . .

"Yes." He grinned suddenly. "Maybe after dinner? This Friday I'm not working late . . . How about I take you out to dinner and then we can salsa a little?"

Her heartbeat sped up. "I'd like that," she said simply. "We can go back to my house afterward and practice there."

"And I'll say hello to your grandmother," he added.

Marisol wanted to skip as he led her back to the table. She would see Alex again soon! Just the two of them!

Of course, he hadn't exactly said it was a date—he'd suggested a private lesson. Still . . . it was close enough.

Alex pulled out her chair and seated her, and she wanted to sigh with pleasure.

"What are you smiling at?" Leo whispered as Alex sat on her other side.

She shot him a glance. "I'm having a good time."

Actually, she thought as she reached for her soda, she was having a spectacular time.

"A private lesson?" Grandma said eagerly. Too eagerly, with a big smile on her face.

"Whoa!" Christa said, grinning.

"Oh!" exclaimed Marisol's mother, Sonya. "So we get a chance to meet this doctor your grandmother has been telling us about?"

Marisol's father, Pedro Senior, just stared in surprise.

Uh-oh. She'd been afraid of these overreactions. "He's

taking me to dinner before that," Marisol said, spooning her grandmother's special *arroz con pollo* from the casserole into her dish while trying to sound ultracasual.

They were seated around the dinner table on Wednesday evening. Marisol had known she had to tell them eventually about Alex, since they'd see him on Friday, so she'd decided to bring it up at dinner. Her fears that her family would read too much into this almost-date were being confirmed. Especially since her grandmother and her parents had been urging her to settle down.

It was times like this when she really wanted her own apartment, a place where her family couldn't interfere and wouldn't know all her comings and goings. It had been nice in college when she lived in the dorms and didn't have her parents checking out all her dates. After coming home and going part time for her master's degree in library science, she'd considered getting her own place. But in her family, girls didn't do that. Her parents had gotten very upset and she'd dropped the idea.

Now she was giving it serious consideration.

"What about Leo?" Marisol's mother asked with a slight frown. She'd hoped from the beginning that Marisol and Leo might get together. "He's a nice, stable man," her mother added.

"Leo isn't exciting enough," Grandma said staunchly.

"Mama!" protested Marisol's mom.

At the same time Christa jumped up and high-fived Grandma. "You got it, *Mamita*!"

"Christa! Mama!" Marisol's mother exclaimed.

Marisol burst out laughing.

Papa smiled. "Sonya," he said quietly, "I believe your mother is right. Leo is a little too . . . too . . ."

"Bland," Christa finished. "Marisol needs someone with more personality."

Marisol rolled her eyes. Really, her family had too many opinions about her life. Although she secretly agreed about Leo. She said nothing, though, afraid to encourage their conjectures.

But did Alex really have more personality? Marisol wondered as they continued to eat, and she fielded their questions about the doctor. She didn't know him well. However, she'd soon find out.

And what did the good doctor think about her?

As they cleared the dishes, she caught her grand-mother's eye. There was a definite twinkle there.

A matchmaking twinkle, Marisol thought.

But she couldn't be mad at her grandmother.

After all, between trying to get Celia interested in Leo—and attempting to get to know Alex herself—wasn't she doing her own matchmaking?

Chapter Three

"So, what are you doing this weekend?" Joyce Ames, one of the library aides, asked Marisol as she sorted a stack of returned children's books on Friday morning.

"I have a date—kind of," Marisol told the older woman. Joyce, who was in her sixties, had worked part time at the library for years, mostly in the children's section. She took a grandmotherly interest in all the employees—and the customers too.

"Kind of . . . ?" she questioned Marisol.

Marisol had been looking at craft books for puppet-making ideas. It was early in June, but school would be out in a few weeks, and then the summer reading program would begin. She'd selected "Magic and Magical Creatures" as this year's theme for the library's summer reading program. She had most of the plans done, with reading, crafts, a couple of movies and even a visiting magician to entertain the children at the once-a-week meetings. Of course, the older children had a different suggested reading list and activities than the younger children. For the six weeks of the program she'd planned age-appropriate activities, and the older children had some summer reading assignments for school that she had to keep track of. But Marisol was really excited about this year's programs. One morning she planned a craft project of making puppets; she just had to narrow down which one of four she wanted to do.

She placed bookmarks in the books for the puppet projects she was considering, and saved the websites for the others, deciding to make her choice over the weekend. As she worked she described her almost date with Alex to Joyce, emphasizing the "private lesson" part.

"Now Marisol," Joyce said, "handsome young men don't ask for private lessons unless they're interested in you personally! He could ask the head teacher if that's all he wanted. But she's in her forties, right, and married?"

"Yes," Marisol said.

"So, he's interested in you!" Joyce finished.

Marisol hoped so!

The day had started slowly, but after school hours, some kids from the junior high came in to finish researching projects. The library was open every evening Monday through Thursday, but closed at five on Fridays and Saturdays, and by four on Sundays. Marisol, though, was only on until four today. And it couldn't come quickly enough.

It was only a twenty-minute ride home to Dover. When she reached her house, she found Grandma in the kitchen, cooking. She'd told her family she was eating out with Alex, but Grandma asked the usual question she voiced when someone was eating out.

"Are you sure you don't want a bite to eat? *Un poco?*"

"Thanks, but no," Marisol replied, "no little bites." She kissed her grandmother, who was stirring spaghetti sauce. Grandma liked to cook Italian food as well as traditional Spanish dishes.

Marisol's parents weren't home from work yet. She hurried upstairs to take a shower and change into a long black skirt and sleeveless red top with sequins at the neck. The day was typical for June, warm and sunny, but becoming muggy. She added a necklace, her favorite gold hoop earrings, and spritzed herself with perfume.

Christa nodded approvingly. "You look great!"

Mama was calling that supper was ready when Marisol heard the doorbell ring, and little Pepé began barking as if he was a Doberman.

Alex was here.

She swallowed and went downstairs, hoping her family didn't ask too many nosy questions. Her mother was more restrained, but Papa might ask questions. And Grandma had become more inquisitive as she grew older.

Papa got to the door before she was downstairs. "Come in," he said cordially.

Alex entered, and Marisol caught her breath.

He wore a dark sports jacket and a stark white shirt,

open at the collar, revealing his golden skin. She had never seen him so dressed up, and the effect was positively dazzling.

Women must fall all over him, she thought.

His eyes met hers, and he smiled.

She smiled back. For tonight, *she* would be the woman at his side.

"Papa, this is Alejandro Lares."

They shook hands, and then her mother and Christa approached, and she introduced them too.

"Dr. Lares!" Grandma pushed through the others, beaming at him as if they had known each other for years. "How wonderful to see you again!"

"I hope you are well, señora?" he asked in his rather formal Spanish, taking her hand and bowing gallantly.

"*Sí, sí*, very well," she said enthusiastically.

Marisol stared at Grandma. If she didn't know better, she might think that her grandmother was flirting with the handsome doctor.

No. It must be her imagination.

With Christa, though, there was no question. Her young cousin was smiling engagingly at Alex.

"You're the doctor who saved *Mamita*!" she enthused.

"Saved? Hardly," Alex replied with a smile.

"Well, practically," Christa went on. "Marisol and José said she was in a lot of pain and you helped her!" Her eyes glowed.

Marisol felt her face growing warm. Really, her family . . .

"Would you like to sit down?" her mother invited.

"Thank you, but we have reservations at Dante's Inferno," Alex said, naming a restaurant that served hot, spicy Italian and Spanish food. It was also one of the most expensive restaurants in the area. Leo, with his frugal ways, had certainly never taken her there!

Marisol noted her mother's eyebrows shoot up, and knew she was impressed. "Well, we won't keep you," she said, and Marisol was pretty sure Alex had just gone up in her mother's estimation. A lot.

Even her father was smiling more widely than usual. "Enjoy yourselves," he told them.

"Have fun!" Christa chimed in.

Mamita smiled her biggest smile.

Marisol wanted to groan.

She left the house with Alex, and he opened the door of his large but modest-looking car. She recognized the insignia of a Volvo.

"I hope Dante's Inferno is all right with you?" he asked as he started the car.

"Perfect," she replied, catching the scent of a subtle but masculine aftershave surrounding Alex.

He asked her about her grandmother as they drove the few minutes to the restaurant.

"She came here from Puerto Rico with her husband and four children in the late 1960s," Marisol told him. "She was pregnant with their fifth child. My mother is her second—her eldest daughter. The owners of the frame and window factory had gone down to Aguada, an area in Puerto Rico where there was high unemployment, and brought back many people to work here. My grandpa was one of them, and he soon became a fore-man." She said it proudly. She'd told the story many times, but each time she was just as proud of her grand-father's hard work and accomplishments.

Alex glanced at her. "I've heard the stories about the two factory owners bringing people up from Puerto Rico. Your grandpa is no longer alive?"

Marisol shook her head. "He died in his sleep one night about five years ago. He'd had a heart attack. Since then, Grandma has lived with us."

"Do you ever go to Puerto Rico?" he asked as he pulled into the restaurant's parking lot.

"I've been there with my family a few times. My uncle Edwin Junior—he's the oldest of my mother's siblings—went to live there with his family many years ago. Grandma and Grandpa used to take their children there once a year when they were little, but our family doesn't go that much." Alex stopped the car, and Marisol wondered whether to open the door herself. She hesi-tated, pleased when Alex came around to open it for her. She gave him a smile and her hand as he helped her out.

She couldn't help marveling how good her hand felt in his.

Once they were seated and had ordered strawberry margaritas, she asked Alex about himself. She was ea-ger to hear about him and his family too.

"Pablo told me your family is from Argentina," she said.

"I was born in Buenos Aires," he said proudly.

"I wondered . . . you have a formal way of speaking," she said.

He smiled. "My mother always says a lot of people don't speak correct Spanish. To her, our way is the correct way."

Marisol laughed. "I have an older brother and sister, who are both married. Christa is my cousin. Do you have brothers or sisters?"

"One older brother," he said as their drinks were served. "My parents came here in the mid-70s. My brother was young, and I was an infant. My father was a businessman who felt there were more opportunities in the United States. He started the appliance store on Blackwell Street, and it's grown now."

"Oh!" Marisol exclaimed. "I know the one. My parents have bought furniture there."

"It's expanded a lot," he said. "My brother is in business with my father now." He held up his glass. "Cheers."

She touched her glass to his. "I guess you didn't want to go into business?" she asked, and sipped her drink. It was icy, fruity, and delicious.

"No." He shook his head, and she noted again how handsome he looked. "I always loved science. I spent a lot of time reading science books, especially about anatomy and physiology."

"I recognized your name . . . everyone knows you were the student who read through the encyclopedia in fifth grade," she said.

"I didn't make it through all the volumes," he told her with a smile.

"Still, that's commendable," she said. "I heard you got a scholarship—to Princeton?"

"Yale," he corrected. "By then, I knew I wanted to help people and combine that with my love of science. But I always wanted to come home to Dover to work . . . even though my parents now live in Hopatcong, near the lake."

"Do you live in Dover now?" she asked.

"No . . . I bought a condo last year in Mt. Arlington." That was a nearby community, not far from her library.

"And what made you decide on emergency medicine?" she asked.

"I thought originally about orthopedics. But during my internship I found I really liked emergency medicine. It's exciting, and there are so many challenges."

He really was a fascinating man, she thought. After ordering their meals, they chatted about their careers, and Marisol was impressed by how dedicated Alex was to his job and his patients. He asked her about what made her become a librarian.

"I thought I wanted to be a teacher," she told him, breaking off a piece of garlic bread. "In college, I decided to take a minor in school library science, since I've always loved to read. Not science, like you. Mostly fiction. Everything from Nancy Drew to the Little House on the Prairie books to Shakespeare and I also liked books about ancient history. Anyway, I discovered I really loved library work, and went for my master's in library science, specializing in children's library services."

"Good for you," he said approvingly. "How did you get into dancing the salsa and teaching?"

"I always liked to dance—ballet and jazz and tap— and last year I realized I missed dancing. I was part of a salsa club in college, so I took a review class and the teacher invited me to help out with the basic class."

As their dinners were served, she asked the question that had been on the tip of her tongue for quite a while— the question she couldn't quite squash.

"So how come you never married?" She tried to make her tone light.

His head shot up, and he looked at her.

"I almost did."

He almost did? Marisol felt something tighten in her stomach.

"What do you mean?" Her voice came out hushed.

He shrugged. "I met Juanita when I was interning. She was a surgical nurse." She heard a wry note in his voice. "I should have realized what her true personality was like when she told me she liked surgery because the patients were unconscious."

Marisol couldn't help a laugh. "She doesn't sound too sympathetic toward them."

"That's exactly right. She wasn't, and I should have realized it." He was frowning as he speared a piece of chicken from his cacciatore. "She didn't really like people. She liked the scientific aspects of nursing, but not the human ones. I finally realized she was . . . very cold. She thought marrying a doctor would be a good deal—almost a business arrangement." He stopped abruptly, as if there was more, but he was reluctant to talk about it.

His eyes looked sad too, and Marisol felt her heart squeeze in empathy.

"I finally called it off," he said. "That was several years ago."

"I'm sorry," she said quietly, and impulsively placed her hand on his.

For a moment, they sat, staring at each other. Marisol was very conscious of her hand on his, his warmth, his serious expression, the dark, romantic atmosphere of the restaurant.

"Thank you." He suddenly turned his hand and grasped hers tightly. She felt warmth shoot up from her hand, through her arm, up to her neck and head. For a moment they regarded each other, hands clasped, and then he withdrew his and went back to eating.

Her heart was now beating erratically.

"You deserve someone better than that, someone who appreciates you—" she stated, then stopped.

Oh no, she thought. She sounded like her mother and grandmother.

But suddenly, Alex was grinning. "That's what my friends said. Not to mention every member of my family."

She relaxed slightly at his flash of humor.

"And you?" he asked suddenly. "Why aren't you married?"

"I'm only twenty-six."

"And I'm thirty-two. So . . . ?"

"I just . . . haven't met the right person, I guess," she said.

"What about that guy Leo? He implied you two were going out."

Marisol stopped herself from saying "Hmph." Instead, she cut a piece of her chicken parmigiana, and replied, "I think of Leo as a friend, that's all. If he has other feelings it's not because I encouraged them."

"Sounds like neither of us is anxious to get married," he said.

She opened her mouth, then closed it.

Maybe Alex wasn't anxious to get married, but . . .

She wasn't exactly in a rush. But she did want to get married, someday. Someday . . . fairly soon.

"Someday," she voiced her thoughts, "I would like to get married and have a family." How many hundreds of times had she daydreamed of reading stories to her own children as she did to the kids at the library?

Alex nodded . . . but said nothing.

Marisol's heart contracted. Didn't he want to marry? Ever?

And why did it bother her so much?

She bent her head, afraid something of her confusion would show in her face.

Alex watched Marisol as she delicately nibbled on a piece of chicken, her face bent momentarily toward her plate. He had seen a flash of something in her expression—something he couldn't quite put his finger on.

He regarded her, marveling that she was so feminine, from the way she looked to her mannerisms. Quite the opposite of Juanita, actually. Juanita had been polished and sleek in a cold sort of way. It was a shame he hadn't realized it sooner.

He didn't want to think about Juanita, or the betrayal he hadn't described to Marisol.

"I was kind of relieved when I broke up with Juanita, actually," Alex admitted, then sat back, wondering why he was sharing that thought with Marisol. Relief was actually only one of several emotions he'd felt.

She looked up, studying him, and he wondered what her thoughts were.

"Relieved?" she repeated.

"Yes. It made me think . . ." He voiced the thought that had been at the back of his mind since that day. "Perhaps I'm just the kind who isn't meant to have a long-term relationship."

Something passed again on her face, a fleeting expression he couldn't decipher. Then she said, slowly, "You thought you weren't meant for a relationship because of one selfish woman?"

He hadn't thought of it exactly that way. "Yes," he said, then found himself watching her closely, curious to see what she'd say.

Her expression had turned indignant. "Please don't assume that all women are like that," she said. "We're not. If you get into a relationship with someone who's nice and kind and"—she paused, as if realizing she sounded very vehement, and then went on in a lighter tone—"well, don't judge all women badly because of one negative experience."

It did give him something to think about. Aloud he said, "I guess I'll try to be more . . . open-minded."

As they finished eating, he noticed that Marisol had become less animated, not withdrawn, exactly, but her usual enthusiasm seemed to have cooled somewhat. Did she think him some kind of antifeminist? His mother, an opinionated woman, had always brought up her sons to believe women were equal, although he knew plenty of Argentinian families who did not hold those beliefs. He should reassure her.

He did, speaking his thoughts aloud.

"Oh. I didn't really believe you were a total male chauvinist," Marisol said.

Which made him wonder what she did believe.

He asked her if she wanted dessert.

"I have flan I made yesterday back at the house," Marisol said. "I thought we'd have some with coffee after we practiced the salsa."

Salsa? With a start he realized he'd been enjoying himself so much he'd forgotten about the private lesson he requested!

"Sounds good to me," he said.

It didn't take long to return to her home. They spoke only a little on the trip back, and Alex wondered why Marisol, who was usually so talkative, seemed somewhat pensive.

When they reached her home, they found her grandmother watching one of the Spanish channels on TV, her foot with the sprained toe propped up on an ottoman. Sitting next to her was an elderly man she introduced as her friend and neighbor, Manuel.

"Christa is downstairs with Laurie," she told Marisol. "And your parents went to the movies. I put up coffee—it's in the kitchen."

"Thanks." Marisol leaned down and hugged her grandmother.

Alex felt a sudden longing. His grandparents had all remained in Argentina, and all died before he finished high school.

"You're lucky you have a grandmother," he said as he trailed after Marisol into the bright and cheery kitchen.

"You don't?" she asked.

"No." Seeing her sympathetic look, he explained that his grandparents were all gone now.

Marisol listened, making consoling murmurs. She thought Alex looked sad as he spoke about his grandparents.

"Come, let's go outside where we have room to move around," Marisol said, "and we can practice the salsa. We can have coffee and dessert after we get our exercise!" She made her voice carefree, although she still felt confused feelings churning inside of her. She'd felt so attracted to Alex, but if he wasn't interested in commitments, well . . . she didn't want to get too close to him. She'd almost ended up with a broken heart once herself.

In college, she'd met Luis, a guy she'd liked immediately. But after a few dates he'd told her he would never get married. His parents were too religious to divorce, but their constant fighting had completely turned him off of long-term relationships. And although Marisol really liked him, and had begun to feel that she could fall in love with him, she'd put a halt to their relationship. She knew she wouldn't change his mind, and she didn't want to end up with a broken heart while trying.

She forced thoughts of Luis away now and brought matches from the kitchen outside with her. Once on the deck she lit two citronella candles. She turned and found Alex regarding her. The evening had turned slightly cooler, but it was still humid, and the sunset was spectacular, all reds and pinks with streaks of purple and gold.

"It's beautiful out here," he said, looking around at the deck, the aboveground pool and the glorious sunset. Her parents had planted flowers that were already blooming—marigolds and impatiens and pansies—and the whole atmosphere in the quiet yard was very romantic.

And it was about to heat up, Marisol thought, as she moved to the small CD player she'd placed outside earlier and switched it on. Immediately, hot salsa music began to play.

"Thank you." She faced Alex. "Do you want to take off your jacket? You'll be more comfortable."

He shrugged out of his jacket, and once again she caught a whiff of his masculine aftershave.

She extended her hand. "Come, salsa with me," she said softly.

He moved closer, and she stepped into his arms. They began the steps of the dance. She fit into his arms so well, she thought, as if they were made for dancing together.

No, she must not think that way.

But she couldn't help it. As they glided around the deck, she felt as if she was a princess in one of the fairy tales she'd enjoyed as a child, dancing with a handsome prince. They danced in perfect unison, and she felt as light as air and just as wonderful as the beautiful June evening, warm and soft and colorful.

"Am I doing all right?" His dark eyes met hers.

"Great. You've really improved since the first class," she said, trying to focus on the here and now, instead of this dreamlike feeling she was experiencing in his arms.

"Thanks." He appeared to be concentrating on his footing.

"Would you like to learn a new variation?" Marisol asked. "You'll be a little ahead of the class since we're going to do it next week."

"That's good. I need the extra practice."

"No, you're doing fine," she said. Apparently, in the area of dancing, Alex didn't have much confidence in himself.

Or in the area of romance, a voice whispered from the back of her brain.

She demonstrated, and they did the steps over and over. Finally, she started the music again and they began dancing from the beginning, adding in the extra steps as she encouraged him.

The steps pulled them slightly apart, and then, breathlessly close. Her gaze met his.

For a moment, she forgot to breathe.

They stared at each other, the moment spinning out, and then she stepped back automatically in time to the music.

But oh! For just a second she had thought he was close enough to kiss her!

They finished the dance, and she felt unusual—not off balance, exactly, just not herself. As if—as if she was not quite steady, her feet not quite on the deck's solid wood floor.

The sun had dropped to the horizon, and the purple twilight shadows grew long around them as they stood, his arm still around her, his hand holding hers, for one taut second.

And then he released her, and she took an unsteady breath.

"You did very well." Her voice was lower than normal, sounding husky to her own ears.

"Thank you." He was studying her, and she wished she could read his expression.

An irritation on her shoulder broke her concentration, and she swatted at a large mosquito. "Ugh," she muttered.

He glanced around. "Don't the citronella candles work?"

"Not completely." She grinned up at him suddenly. "Must be my hot Latin blood."

"Either that, or the mosquitoes love you because you're sweet." He smiled at her suddenly, then bent forward.

"I'd want to taste you if I was a mosquito," he whispered, and then kissed her shoulder.

His lips were warm and smooth against her skin.

Marisol felt hot, yet she wanted to shiver with delight. How could a light kiss—on her shoulder—cause such a volcanic reaction inside her?

He lifted his head, and his eyes met hers. His lips moved closer . . .

"Marisol!" It was Christa's voice form the kitchen. "Can Laurie and I have some flan?"

Ohh! Her family . . . !

Alex stepped back, and Marisol blew out a breath. She wanted to groan. What a moment for someone to interrupt! She was going to kill her cousin.

He had almost kissed Marisol Acevedo.

He had wanted to . . . *mucho.*

Alejandro sighed as he drove on the highway, the radio tuned to a quiet jazz station.

It had been a delightful evening. He'd enjoyed Marisol's company, and the time had flown. The dance lesson he'd almost forgotten had been—he could admit it to himself—fun. He was beginning to get the hang of this salsa thing, he'd thought proudly.

But then—the atmosphere had changed. And what had started as a simple and lively dance session had turned into a sensual moment. He hadn't thought, he'd just acted, letting his lips brush Marisol's velvety soft shoulder. And then—he'd wanted to kiss her. Yearned to kiss her.

Until her cousin had called out, breaking the charged atmosphere.

There'd been no time alone after that. Part of him regretted that fact—a lot. But part of him was relieved. He wasn't sure he was ready for anything more than a casual relationship—with anyone.

Marisol's cousin Christa had come out, then stopped short, obviously realizing she had stumbled on an intimate moment. She'd stuttered an apology, but by then he and Marisol had moved apart. And Marisol had suggested, her color rosy, that they have their flan. Which turned out to be delicious.

Besides her cousin Christa and Christa's friend, they'd been joined by Marisol's grandmother and her friend, Manuel. And though he'd enjoyed the light-hearted conversation, he'd wished for more time with Marisol . . . alone. Which was a contradiction to what he thought he should be feeling. Shouldn't he want to keep things light and carefree? Being in the company of Marisol's relatives and their friends would accomplish that.

Alex turned off the highway onto the main road that led to his condo development, sighing again. He'd put in a full day of work before seeing Marisol, but instead of being tired, he felt energized. The evening had been fun and he knew he wanted to see Marisol again.

But was that a good idea?

The only other moment he'd had alone with Marisol was when he'd left and she'd stood by the door with him. Her cousin's friend had departed and her cousin had disappeared upstairs; and Margarita and Manuel were still in the kitchen, conversing at the table about the show they'd been watching on TV.

"I'd like to see you again," he'd practically blurted out as he stood looking at Marisol's lovely face. He winced now, thinking he'd sounded like a teenager. Not to mention the fact that he'd spoken without thinking, which was unusual for Alejandro Lares.

"I'd like that," she'd murmured in return.

Conscious that others were nearby, he'd given her a very quick, casual hug.

"I'll see you in class on Tuesday," he'd whispered, and touched her cheek with a finger. Her cheek was silky soft. "And we can make plans to get together."

She'd nodded, her eyes fastened on him. And he'd smiled and left.

He turned now into the side street and proceeded to enter the condo development, making two swift turns that brought him to his parking space. He shut off the car, then exited.

Why on earth did Marisol Acevedo bring out all these contradictory feelings in him? he wondered.

Marisol curled up on the couch, reached for the TV remote, and listlessly flipped through different channels.

The house was unnaturally quiet this Saturday night.

Mamita was at a senior citizens' party at the church. Marisol's parents were at a neighbor's for the evening.

Christa was at a party at a friend's house. Even Pepé, curled on his favorite chair, was sound asleep.

"You're going to stay home alone?" Marisol's mother had asked an hour before, frowning slightly.

"There's nothing wrong with that," Marisol had defended. "I went out yesterday with Alex. I don't have to go out every night on a weekend."

"But won't you be bored?" her mother had pressed.

Marisol knew her real concern was, won't you be lonely?

"I have a new book to read." She had patted the cover of a romance novel by one of her favorite authors.

"What about Carina?" her mother had continued. "Or Celia?"

Her best friend from high school was busy, going out for the third time with a guy she liked. "Carina has a date," Marisol had told her mother. "And Celia's visiting cousins in Hoboken."

"You could always call Leo."

"No, I don't think so," Marisol had stated. She didn't want to get into it with her mother, but she was not calling Leo. That would definitely give him the wrong idea, when she was hoping to show him she didn't want anything more than a friendly relationship with him. "Don't worry," she had added, smiling at her mom. "I'm planning on a nice, quiet evening to myself. The library was very busy this week."

"Well . . . okay," her mother had said, still looking doubtful.

"Leave her alone," her father had chided suddenly, coming in from the kitchen. "If my daughter doesn't want to go out, she doesn't have to."

So they'd departed, leaving the house strangely quiet. Marisol had taken Pepé for a walk, but dark clouds were rolling in, and they'd returned shortly to the house.

Where she now sat on the couch, thinking of Alex.

Since last night, she'd barely been able to stop thinking of him. She knew she was drawn to Alejandro Lares. He was personable and intelligent and wryly funny.

But it sounded like he didn't want a long-term relationship. So was she wasting her time spending it with someone who said he wasn't anxious to get married?

Yet how could she not spend time with him? She enjoyed the time they spent together. A lot. She wanted to keep seeing him.

And he'd already said he wanted to see her again.

She sighed, turned off the TV, and reached for her romance novel.

She would just have to wait and see what developed.

Chapter Four

"That's it for tonight, people!" Sondra said, clapping her hands enthusiastically. "Give yourselves a round of applause. You all did very well!"

As everyone obeyed her instructions and applauded their dancing efforts, Alex moved slowly toward the front where Marisol was standing.

He'd hardly gotten a word in with her during class or the breaks. The steps were getting more difficult, and a lot of people had required her help tonight. Since she had gone over the variations with him last week, he'd been able to keep up. He almost wished he hadn't done so well. He'd love a little of the attention she was giving to some of the other students.

But he shouldn't be selfish, he reminded himself. He was going to ask Marisol out again, and then he'd have her full attention.

He hung back as people began leaving. Irena had gone around to everyone in what she called "the group" during their break to tell them to meet after class and discuss getting together this weekend.

As Irena pulled his cousin Pablo over toward Dominick and Anne, Alex questioned, not for the first time, how good she was for Pablo. She was rather bossy, he'd always thought, and seeing her now, trying to manage the group that had gotten together last week, he wondered why her bossiness wasn't grating on Pablo's nerves. Or maybe it was. His cousin *was* looking annoyed.

He followed and caught up to his cousin. Touching Pablo's arm, he said to him in a low voice, "Do you really want to get together with all these people?"

Pablo looked startled. He paused, and Alex knew his cousin well enough to know he was considering his answer. Then, he replied, "Yes." He must have seen Alex's surprise, because he dropped his voice further. "It's not the idea that bothers me . . . it's just . . . Irena didn't bother to ask me first."

Alex nodded, but was unable to reply as Irena was approaching.

The others soon joined their little group, and they began debating where to go over the weekend.

"Are you working?" Irena asked Alex, knowing that his schedule often changed from week to week.

"Friday night, yes, but not Saturday," he said.

"Good! Saturday it is." She clapped her hands and looked over as Marisol and Celia, done with their straightening up, joined them.

"What about going to the movies?" someone suggested. Alex was barely paying attention. He was focused on Marisol.

She looked gorgeous in a simple lemon yellow dress. It set off her tan and dark hair and she easily outshone the other women there.

There was some debate, and people seemed to be concluding that there wasn't too much to see, since half of them had already seen the latest superhero adventure. He hardly listened.

Marisol had caught his eye, and was giving him her wide, generous smile.

Her smile did something to him. It warmed him, and made him want to laugh, and . . . he caught himself. What the heck was going on with him? He never had thoughts like those. A simple smile didn't just make someone want to laugh out loud.

But it did. She did. There was something—he couldn't figure out what—about Marisol that made people feel good and carefree. It was as if she thought the world was an absolutely wonderful place and by smiling, she could make you think so too.

They could definitely use some of that attitude in the emergency room, he thought wryly.

"Well, what else is going on?" Irena asked, frowning.

"The carnival, yes?" Marisol exclaimed.

"Perfect," Celia cried.

"Yes!" several others echoed.

The next town over had a carnival every June on the field behind their firehouse, complete with rides, games, cotton candy and all the usual attractions. It had been going on forever. Alex had gone with his parents when he was young, and later as a teenager, with his friends. When he was older he'd been too busy with his studies. It was all right, if you liked that kind of thing. He was sure there were other activities he'd prefer.

Everyone was nodding and agreeing with enthusiasm. Irena turned to him abruptly.

"Well, Alex?" she asked.

He stared at her for a moment. "Well?"

"What do you think?" she said.

He must have been the only one who hadn't responded. Beyond her, he saw Marisol staring at him. She looked hopeful.

"It will be fun, *amigo*," Xavier said.

"Okay," Alex said, wondering how much fun it would be.

But then he saw Marisol's smile again, lighting up her face.

Maybe it would be fun?

Saturday was sunny and in the high eighties. Marisol didn't have to work, so she started the day with a shopping excursion with Christa. Christa wanted a couple of new things for the summer, since school would be out soon, and Marisol wanted to treat herself to some new clothes too.

She especially wanted to find something to wear for the evening. Something casual and pretty.

She'd found exactly what she wanted. Now she

dressed in the new tan capri pants and turquoise sleeveless top she'd bought. She added a multicolored bead necklace and coppery bracelet. She had a dark brown zipped sweatshirt she could bring along, in case the evening got cool when the sun went down. She quickly put on makeup and brushed her hair, and was slipping into her comfortable, flat sandals when Christa entered the room.

"You look great!" her cousin said enthusiastically.

"Thanks." Marisol smiled at her fondly. Christa had apologized more than once for interrupting her time with Alex last week, and Marisol was amused to see how serious her teenage cousin was about the fact that she was going out with Alex. Obviously he'd made a good impression on her.

And on everyone else. Grandma had said a few days ago that she liked the young doctor and hoped she'd see him again. Even Marisol's mother, who tended to be fussy, had admitted she thought Alejandro was nice.

"And a good catch," she'd added.

Marisol had shrugged off that comment. "I'm just going out with him to have fun." At least that's what she kept telling herself.

She glanced at her watch now. He should be here in a few minutes.

He'd surprised her by calling her on her cell phone only minutes after she'd gotten home from class on Tuesday. Their "group" had agreed to meet at the front entrance to the carnival at seven o'clock. But then Alex had called, asking Marisol if she'd go with him.

And she'd instantly answered yes.

"You're going to have fun!" Christa told her now, eyes gleaming. She'd been to the carnival last night with a bunch of her friends. "Make him go on a scary ride with you, so you can scream and hang on to him."

Marisol laughed. "I'll keep that idea in mind."

The doorbell rang as she was walking down the stairs, and Pepé began barking like a maniac.

Marisol opened it. It was Alex, a few minutes early.

He was dressed in jeans and a plain black T-shirt, yet he managed to look like a movie star in his simple clothes.

"*Hola,* Alejandro," she greeted him, marveling that she was able to keep her voice light. The man was striking.

He stared at her for a moment, then smiled.

"*Bonita,*" he said, his voice husky. "Always, you look beautiful, Marisol."

A warm rush of pleasure at his words sped through her. "*Muchas gracias,*" she thanked him. "You look good yourself!" She tried to make the words light, but they stuck in her throat. He was more than good-looking. She could see him posing for the cover of the romance novels she liked to read.

Pepé was jumping at Alex, wagging his tail and barking. Alex bent to pet the little dog. "Good boy."

"Okay, Pepé," Marisol said, and he turned to jump at her. Then he turned back to Alex. Obviously, Alex was a big favorite.

She was glad to see that Alex was patient with Pepé

as his prancing and barking continued. Alex went up further in her estimation.

Before she could suggest leaving, she heard footsteps, and her grandmother approached.

"Alejandro, I am glad to see you," she said.

He smiled. "A pleasure, *señora*."

"Shall we go?" Marisol suggested, before the rest of her family crowded in. Christa was leaving soon for a sleepover at a friend's house, but Grandma and her parents were around, although Marisol knew they were all going out later—her parents to her uncle's house, and her grandmother to play cards with Manuel and some other friends.

"It may be cool later," Alex said. "You should bring a sweater."

She held up her sweatshirt. "Thanks. I'll bring this along."

She called good-bye to everyone and they departed.

She couldn't help but feel excited as they drove the short distance to the carnival grounds. It was always a fun event, but being in Alex's company would make it even more so.

A policeman was directing traffic and indicated parking in an adjoining field. They bumped their way over the uneven grassy surface, chatting about their work weeks. Alex had had patients with everything from a gall bladder attack to a woman who had been shot by her estranged husband—not fatally, fortunately.

Marisol told him how she had scrambled to finish getting ready for the summer reading program. She noticed that the field was getting pretty full already, although the carnival hadn't opened till six o'clock. Alex was directed by another officer to pull into a specific space.

"What do they do when there's no parking left?" Alex asked, opening the car door for her.

Marisol wanted to sigh with pleasure. What a gentleman! "They have people park by the elementary school and the other fields, and bus them over here." She gave him her hand and exited his car.

Alex reached past her, grabbed a gray sweatshirt, and tied the sleeves around his waist. Marisol did the same with hers and he extended his hand.

"Let's go," he said cheerfully.

They approached the entrance to the carnival. Marisol spotted Irena and Pablo, Anne and Dominick and Celia there already.

They didn't have to wait long until Xavier, Leo, and Shannon joined them. They paid, with Alex insisting on paying for Marisol, and entered the carnival grounds.

Instantly, Marisol was engulfed by the sights, smells, and sounds of the carnival, which hadn't changed much since she was a child. The whooshing sound of different rides with squealing passengers; the bright neon lights flashing over the games; and the appealing smell of hot popcorn were all familiar to her senses.

"Let's try the Ferris wheel," Irena suggested.

The others tagged along as she led the way to the Ferris wheel in the back. It was warm right now, with the sun still out. Marisol watched as Celia, in a rather flamboyant outfit, walked in front of her. Celia wore a low-necked burgundy top and short denim skirt. Her sandals had heels and although they were pretty, Marisol wondered how she could walk in them over the uneven ground.

This Ferris wheel appeared to be a small one, Marisol noted with relief. She didn't care for heights. She would go on this Ferris wheel, but never went on the really high ones.

"I like that ride," Marisol said, pointing to the tilt-a-whirl as they passed it.

Alex raised his eyebrows. "You like fast rides?"

"Some of them, yes," Marisol said.

Their tickets allowed them to go on unlimited rides. The Ferris wheel line was short, and although Leo sidled up near them, Marisol stepped closer to Alex.

The Ferris wheel paused and Anne and Dominick were the first of their group to climb aboard. It revolved upward, and then Alex and Marisol sat in the next seat.

"We'll get a nice view of the carnival," Alex said as they were lifted. Marisol was pleased to see Celia and Leo got into the next chair. Maybe they really would hit it off.

"Hmm . . ." Marisol murmured. Now that she was on the Ferris wheel, it seemed higher than it had looked from the entrance. She tried to think about Celia and Leo.

They rose slowly as more people got on. As they neared the top, Marisol sat back in the seat, trying not to look down.

Alex glanced at her, and then the Ferris wheel began to move.

Marisol swallowed, looking at her knees.

"Marisol?" Alex's voice was quiet. "Are you all right?"

"I—I don't like heights," she admitted.

"You should have said something. We didn't have to come on this ride—" He stopped, then abruptly scooted closer. Wrapping one arm around Marisol's shoulders, he pulled her close. "Don't look down," he said.

She burrowed her head into his shoulder. "Okay, I won't." She stared instead at his neck, breathing in his masculine, slightly spicy aftershave.

His lips brushed the top of her hair, and despite being scared, Marisol felt a shiver of delight.

"You can look at me," he said. He sounded slightly amused. "I take it you're not scared of all the rides?"

"I'm only scared of the high ones," she said. Their chair swung and she refused to look down, concentrating instead on his neck, his dark skin glowing with a slight tan.

She could feel him smiling against her forehead. "It's all right," he said soothingly. "It will be over soon."

This must be the way he calms patients, she thought. The chair moved downward, then she could feel them swooping upward again. She pressed her face against his neck, harder. She didn't want to look.

Her hands were tightly gripping the metal bar. He reached out, covering her hands with his larger one, and smoothed his thumb over her knuckles. "It's all right," he repeated softly. "*Querida,* don't be scared." Then in Spanish he added, "Have no fear. I would never let anything happen to you."

Marisol drew in a sharp breath—not from fear, but from the thrill that swept through her. He had called her sweetheart!

He continued to stroke her knuckles as the chair moved upward, then swung down again in a rhythmic motion. She felt her hands relaxing. For the first time, the tightness in her stomach that had been present since they got on the Ferris wheel began to ease.

She was with Alejandro Lares. And he would never let anything happen to her.

She stayed pressed against his side, her face buried in his neck. He had one arm around her shoulders and the other hand stroking her hands, as the Ferris wheel swooped up, then down, several times. And then the ride slowed, and people began to get out.

"We're next," Alex whispered into her ear.

She slowly sat up, seeing that they were close to the ground. She glanced up at him to see Alex was looking at her with affection.

"That wasn't so bad, no?" he asked as their chair lowered to the ground.

"No," she whispered, gazing at him. "Because I was with you."

Alex grinned and the man on the ground opened the safety bars. Alex gripped Marisol's elbow as they disembarked.

They gathered together with the others, but he kept his hand lightly on her elbow. Marisol felt its warmth and shot him a grateful smile. He'd made the Ferris wheel ride an almost comfortable experience for her.

"Where to next?" Shannon was asking.

Marisol suggested the tilt-a-whirl. Shannon and Xavier agreed, but the others wanted to try the roller coaster, which was a pretty high one. They split up, agreeing to meet in an hour by the carousel.

Marisol and Alex walked behind Shannon and Xavier. The other couple appeared to be getting along well, and Marisol thought she saw sparks of interest in both their eyes. Had their class started a romance, she wondered?

"I wanted to ask you," Alex began, and hesitated.

"Yes?" Marisol asked, looking up at him. The evening air was soft and warm, punctuated by the noise and commotion of the carnival, and the sky still bright.

"My mother still likes to make a formal early dinner on most Sundays." He looked at her as though he was uncertain of her reaction. "Would you like to join us?"

Would she? An invitation to a family event! Marisol smiled as she gazed up at him. "I'd be delighted. Can I bring something—dessert or something?"

"No, that's not necessary," Alex assured her.

Following her delight was a quick burst of anxiety. She would meet Alex's parents—what would they think of her? Would they be looking at her critically? She imagined they were a little more serious than her family, since Alex was a more serious person. What if they didn't like her?

"My brother, Juan Carlos, and his wife, Maria, will be there," he continued, "along with their two-year-old son and my great aunt—my grandfather's sister."

She hoped Alex hadn't—she glanced at him.

His mouth was suddenly set in a firm line. He'd obviously seen who his cousin was kissing—a woman who was not his fiancée.

A woman who was Marisol's coworker and friend.

Chapter Five

Alex pulled Marisol down the path before the couple noticed them.

Marisol swallowed.

"I'm sorry," she said when they were back on the main street.

Alex shook his head. "You have nothing to be sorry about."

"True, but—I feel bad anyway."

Alex's face had taken on a stony expression.

"What . . . what do you want to do?" Marisol whispered. She hoped he wasn't going to make a big thing about it.

Although it had looked like Celia and Pablo were making a big deal over each other. That had been no quick kiss. That had been a hungry, desperate kiss—

Alex interrupted her thoughts. "Nothing. My cousin—

that's his business." He frowned. "Although I think he's wrong to do what he did—that's between him and Irena. I'm not going to say anything to her."

Marisol nodded. "I think that's the best thing to do." But oh! She felt bad. Bad that her friend was fooling around with Alex's cousin—a cousin who was supposed to be marrying someone else soon. And bad that Alex had lost that happy look on his face, and now seemed concerned and preoccupied.

They walked for a moment in silence. "I have to admit, I'm surprised," Marisol said in a low voice. She hoped if they talked about it maybe Alex wouldn't look so tense.

"Obviously, Celia can't be trusted," Alex said tersely.

Why would he assume the woman was to blame? "Or Pablo," Marisol retorted.

He shot her a look, and his face took on an apologetic expression. "I'm sorry. I shouldn't have said that. Or Pablo," he added. "I guess it's hard to admit my cousin could be—cheating."

Marisol felt her stiff spine relax. "Apology accepted."

But inside she still felt tense. Because it seemed obvious that Alex really didn't trust women. Her mind flew back to his mention of his ex-fiancée, Juanita. Was there more to the story than he'd told her originally? She'd bet there was. Maybe Juanita couldn't be trusted?

And now, after seeing Celia . . . would he lose the trust she thought he was beginning to have? The trust he had been feeling toward her, she had hoped?

If he did revert to not trusting women—which she

doubted he even was aware of—that didn't bode well for their relationship.

He had turned to look straight ahead, and his mouth was still unsmiling. She moved closer to him.

But though he still held on to her hand, his grip was less firm than it had been just minutes before.

"It's almost time to head back to the carousel," Alex said.

They walked down the uneven street, the thuds and squeals from the bumper car ride they were passing punctuating their silence.

Ahead they saw Anne and Dominick, eating ice cream cones. Anne waved at them.

"We were just heading back to the carousel," she said. "Where is everyone?"

Alex shrugged, and Marisol said, "We were with Xavier and Shannon, but we lost track of them."

Anne was smiling. "I kind of think there's something going on there."

Ha! And not only there! Marisol thought.

Would anyone else notice that Celia and Pablo had somehow ended up together? She hoped not.

Dominick suggested they ride the carousel, when they got there a few minutes early. They went around, and Marisol would have enjoyed the ride on a golden-colored horse beside Alex, if he hadn't looked so tense.

When they got off, the rest of the crowd was already there. Marisol hadn't seen if Celia and Pablo had joined the others together or separately. She hoped they had come from different directions.

Irena was busy talking to Shannon and Xavier, and Leo and Pablo were chatting. Celia stood slightly behind Shannon, but Marisol noticed she was flushed and her straight, light brown hair appeared mussed.

Marisol moved over closer to Celia. She wasn't going to say anything, but . . .

Alex, she noticed, hung back a bit, then moved closer to Pablo.

She wanted to groan. She hoped he didn't perceive this as taking sides.

"Let's get on line," Irena commanded, and led the way to the short line for the carousel.

Marisol couldn't help noticing the slight grimace on Pablo's face as he followed her slowly.

Shannon and Xavier followed Irena and Pablo and scooted onto one of the carousel's benches, sitting close together. Marisol returned to the golden horse, and Alex climbed on the blue one next to her. He appeared to have carefully schooled his features into a neutral expression.

As the carousel turned and her horse bobbed up and down, Marisol found herself studying Alex. What was he thinking?

He turned and met her gaze.

Leaning toward her, he said softly, "Don't worry. I am hoping this—aberration—will work itself out."

Marisol nodded. But inside, she felt like her stomach was still in knots. She had seen that expression on Pablo's face. Was he getting tired of his fiancée's bossy ways? Was that little interlude with Celia a rebellion on Pablo's part against Irena's control?

The carousel slowed. They filed off, and Marisol was right behind Shannon and Xavier as he put his arm around the younger woman's shoulders.

Pablo made no such gesture with Irena.

Dominick and Anne too, had their arms wrapped around each other.

"Let's try the bumper cars," Irena said.

"We did that already," Dominick protested.

"Well, how about the swings?" Irena asked.

Several people had tried those too, but were willing to go on them again. Marisol shook her head.

Alex stood right behind her. She turned slightly. "You can try them," she suggested. "I'll watch."

Alex shook his head. "No, I'll stay with you. We can watch together."

Warmth crept up her spine, and she smiled at him.

They all started down the main street. It was getting darker now, and lights began to appear on some corners and at a few of the rides.

Marisol and Alex found a bench to sit on while the others got on the swings. The others whirled around, the whole ride tilting at an angle and going higher and higher. There were shrieks and laughs, but Marisol was glad her feet were planted firmly on the ground. She smelled popcorn, closer this time, and nearby neon green and pink lights blinked over the carnival games.

Alex sat close on the bench, but not as close as they'd been on the rides. She moved infinitesimally closer, turning to study him.

His face wore a brooding expression. Abruptly he turned, conscious that Marisol was looking at him.

"Sorry," he said hastily. "My mind was miles away."

Marisol bit her lip, refraining from asking what he was thinking about.

Was he thinking about his past? His cousin's love life alone wouldn't have him this upset, she guessed.

Their friends were getting off the ride, some of them wobbling over the rutted grass and pathways. Shannon appeared unsteady, and so did Celia.

Celia tripped and plunged to the ground. "Oh!" she shrieked.

Marisol jumped up and ran over to her friend as the others turned and gathered close.

Xavier, who was closest to Celia, was already on one knee. "Are you all right?" he asked.

Celia struggled to sit up. "I'm ok—oww!"

Her face was flushed and she had tears in her eyes, whether from pain or embarrassment Marisol couldn't tell. She reached her and dropped down beside Xavier.

"Are you hurt?" she asked her.

Celia brushed at a streak of dirt across her leg, bending her head. "I don't know."

"Here." Xavier helped pull Celia up, but she moaned.

"Let me take a look," Alex said, pushing past a few others.

"Yes, he's a doctor, let him check you," Irena urged.

Alex and Xavier lowered Celia to the ground. A crowd was gathering, and Marisol watched as Alex examined

Celia. He held her foot gently, probing slightly with his fingers. Celia winced.

Marisol couldn't help admire how Alex was conducting himself. Despite any lingering feelings of resentment or distrust toward Celia, he was being careful and gentle, asking her questions about whether it hurt here, or there, in a nice calm voice. Finally he looked up.

"I don't think anything's broken," he said. "It looks like a sprain, but we better have it X-rayed and checked."

Someone from the carnival had come over. "Should we call the emergency squad? They're right nearby," the man said.

"No, no," Celia said hastily. "I'm fine, really. Help me up." Alex and Xavier complied as the man went to get a disposable ice pack for Celia.

"Those shoes are too high for this rough ground," Irena pointed out in a know-it-all voice that Marisol found irritating.

Celia made a face. "I know that now."

"I think you should have this X-rayed," Alex repeated.

"No, it's not so bad now," Celia said. "I'll go home and rest. If it still hurts later I'll have my father take me to the emergency room."

Alex started to protest, but Celia was insistent. "Really. I think I can walk." She glanced over at Shannon. "Would you mind bringing me home? Shannon and I came together," she explained to the group.

"Of course not," Shannon said, although she glanced quickly at Xavier.

Xavier started to speak, when Pablo said, "I can drive you home."

"No," Alex interrupted. "We'll take her." He glanced at Marisol. "Is that okay with you?'

"Of course," Marisol answered. She was perfectly aware that Alex was trying to avoid the circumstance of his cousin spending more time with her friend.

They helped Celia, who hobbled along without comment. As they left the others, Pablo called out, "Let us know how you're feeling."

"Okay," Celia responded faintly.

They said little. Once they reached the entrance to the field, Alex went to get his car, explaining to the officer what was going on so they'd let him pull up close.

As he strode away, Celia said to Marisol, her voice pitched low, "You saw us, didn't you?"

There was no sense in denying it. "Yes," Marisol said, and sighed.

"Please don't think badly of me," Celia said, shifting her position so her weight was on her other foot. Marisol put an arm around her friend, supporting her.

"It's just that—I've had this—crush—on Pablo since the first class," Celia continued. "He's so sweet, so handsome—and so kind. But I didn't encourage him, I swear it—I'd never try to break him and Irena up. I thought the crush was the kind of thing that would go nowhere, I'd get over it, you know?"

Marisol nodded. She'd never known Celia to try to steal someone's boyfriend—it would be out of character for her friend. She just wasn't that type.

"Then—I'm not sure how—some of our group wanted to go on the roller coaster again. Pablo and I didn't want to, so we decided to play some of the carnival games. After a little while, we were talking, and suddenly he said"—she paused, then continued, her voice lower—"he said that he couldn't stop thinking about me, and all he wanted to do was kiss me—and then—somehow we *were* kissing—" She stopped.

"Did anyone else see you?" Marisol asked.

"I don't think so. After he kissed me, he apologized, and then—he thought we should head back to the carousel separately. So I went to the ladies' room"—she pointed to the back of the firehouse—"and by the time I got back to the carousel, everyone else was there." Her cheeks were stained a rosy color. "Honestly, Marisol, I'd never—"

"Here comes Alex," Marisol said, spotting his car. "I know, Celia, you wouldn't encourage an engaged man. Especially one engaged to Irena," she said dryly, trying to add some humor to the situation. "She'd have your head."

Celia didn't answer, just nodded.

Alex helped Celia into the backseat, and she gave him directions to her home. They drove, listening to a local rock music station, with Marisol and Celia making light remarks about the carnival rides and games.

Alex said little.

They both helped her into her house. No one else was home at the time, so they left her on the couch, her foot propped up with pillows, and aspirin and a glass of water beside her.

Marisol tactfully avoided the subject of the kiss they'd witnessed on the way back to her house. Once there, she invited Alex in, but he declined.

"I worked late yesterday—we had some emergencies that caused me to stay beyond my regular hours," he told her. "I'm kind of tired. But," he added, brushing her hair back from her face, "I'll see you tomorrow."

She had almost forgotten that she was going to his parents' tomorrow.

"What's their address?" she asked.

"I'll pick you up—is two o'clock okay?" he asked.

"Fine." She regarded him. His fingers were playing with her hair, and he said suddenly, "Your hair is so soft—like silk. I love the way it feels."

Warmth rushed through her, like an ocean wave. "Thanks," she whispered.

He bent his head, and kissed her gently on the lips.

It still made her almost as dizzy as the carnival rides.

What had he been thinking?

As Alex drove to Marisol's house on Sunday, he wondered again why he had just blurted out the invitation to dinner. It certainly wasn't a habit of his to invite beautiful women over to dinner.

He'd been toying with the idea of introducing Marisol to his family. And at last Sunday's dinner—his family had gone to Pablo's parents', and he joined them all after work—Pablo had mentioned something about Marisol to Alex's brother, Juan Carlos.

"Alex is dating a special girl?" Great-Aunt Teresa,

never one to miss an opportunity for hot news, had questioned.

Alex's mother had sent him a surprised look.

The whole family's attention had centered on Alex then.

"Alejandro, do you have a girlfriend?" his mother had asked.

"Not exactly," he'd hedged. Did all families think it was their mission to know everything about your personal life, or was this just his family's goal?

"Tell us about her," his brother, Juan Carlos, had said.

"She's gorgeous," Pablo had added.

"Really?" Alex's father grinned.

Alex had explained that he'd taken Marisol out but she was *not* his girlfriend.

"The way you were looking at her in class this week, man—" Pablo started.

"In class?" asked Aunt Teresa eagerly.

"Hush," Irena said, playfully hitting Pablo. "Maybe he doesn't want to talk about it."

He'd been bombarded with questions after Pablo's statement. He'd managed to answer briefly, reiterating that he'd only taken Marisol out once.

His mother and Pablo's mother had exchanged long glances.

Then he'd steered the conversation back to learning the salsa for Pablo's wedding. And that, he'd thought, was the end of it.

Until the invitation to Sunday dinner just seemed to pop out of his mouth yesterday.

Marisol had seemed eager to accept.

But now he was having second—and third—thoughts.

After this visit, his family would know he really was dating Marisol. He hadn't brought a girl home for dinner in—he couldn't remember how long. Not since Juanita, he suspected, and he'd been dating Juanita for months before he'd asked her to meet his family.

And now, on top of that, there was this uncomfortable situation with Pablo—and Celia. A situation that he hoped was a onetime, never-to-occur-again type of thing. But it didn't bode well for Pablo's future marriage.

Alex sighed and attempted to push his cousin's problems to the back of his brain.

That same brain went right back to thinking about Marisol.

It's just a dinner, he assured himself as he turned off the main highway.

Since he hadn't worked this morning, he'd attended church with his parents. After the Mass, he'd casually slipped in that he hoped his mother didn't mind, but he had invited a friend for dinner.

"Of course I don't mind," his mother had said. Her sharp eyes studied him. "Which friend?"

"A female friend?" Aunt Teresa asked eagerly. She lived nearby, and always accompanied them to church and came over afterward.

"Yes. Marisol Acevedo . . . the dance instructor," he said. "The woman I mentioned last week."

"The one Pablo was speaking of," his mother said, her expression neutral.

"The gorgeous one?" his father asked.

Alex had sighed, the sound unusually loud. His mother had frowned.

They'd reached their car by then. As Alex went to open the door for his aunt, he heard his mother whisper to his father, "He hasn't brought a girl home since Juanita."

"It's about time he did again," his father answered, more loudly.

Alex had changed the topic after that.

Now he turned down one street, then another, approaching Marisol's home. This was not the neighborhood he'd grown up in. His parents had owned a home in the north section of town, where the houses stood on larger lots and the neighborhood was considered more prestigious. Several years ago Juan Carlos and Maria had bought his childhood home from his parents, and his parents had bought a house in Hopatcong, near the lake. With Juan Carlos in business his father could spend more time on his boat, which he really loved.

He parked on the street in front of Marisol's house and got out. The day was warm, but not unbearable. An air conditioner hummed in the Acevedos' front window, and across the street several children were playing with some kind of sprinkler toy that squirted water. The children ran through the water, laughing.

The minute he rang the bell Marisol's dog started barking. The door opened, and Marisol greeted him. "Come on in."

She looked as pretty as always. She wore black pants

and a gold, silky short-sleeved shirt that had an oriental style. Gold hoop earrings peeked through her silky black hair, and a light floral scent surrounded her.

"*Hola,* Dr. Lares," Margarita Soto said from behind Marisol.

"How is your foot, *señora?*" he asked as he entered the house.

"Better. It is almost normal now," she said, beaming at him.

Marisol watched as her grandmother talked to Alex. It was obvious that *Mamita* liked and approved of him. Within a minute, Marisol's father and mother had come over to greet him too, their expressions welcoming.

Marisol wanted to groan. Did they have to make their approval of her date so obvious? It had been apparent from the first that her grandmother had liked the young doctor. Her father had followed. And since Alex had taken her to eat at Dante's Inferno, Marisol noticed Alex had gone up in her mother's estimation too. Her mother had stopped asking about Leo and now asked every couple of days about Alex.

"And wasn't the carnival cool?" Christa was asking. She too, thought he was great boyfriend material.

At least Christa wasn't constantly urging her to get married, Marisol thought. But her teenage cousin had said quite a few times that Alex was "hot."

"Um . . . we'd better get going," Marisol said, picking up her purse.

She managed to maneuver them out in another minute, and then they were on their way to Alex's parents' house.

Marisol had tried to dress up a bit for Sunday dinner, but to dress conservatively. Her top had short sleeves but a collar. She had kept her jewelry simple. She suspected that meals at Alex's house might be more formal than Sunday dinners at her house. Her best friend from high school, Carina, was Mexican, and her family's Sunday dinners, while as full of food as the Acevedos' meals, were more formal affairs. From what Marisol had observed, her friends from South America were even more formal.

She listened as Alex told her who would be there. His father's widowed aunt Teresa, who had come to this country with her husband a few years after Alex's family. They'd never been able to have children, so she regarded Alex's father and uncle like her own. Alex's brother, Juan Carlos, and his wife, Maria, who had been born in Chile, would be there, plus their two-year-old son, Matthew.

Marisol wondered if they'd all be studying her.

Alex drove into the hills of Hopatcong, deftly turning the car on roads that were narrower and more hilly than Dover's. Finally he slowed, and pulled into a driveway. "Here we are."

The house was a nice-size ranch, white with black shutters. The lawn outside was well-kept, and flowers lined the path to the door.

He unlocked the door and then ushered her inside. The house was nice and cool. They must have central air-conditioning, she thought. They were in a wide hallway, and on the left was a large living room, tastefully decorated in tones of pale green and cream, with touches of gold, the furniture large and new-looking. Sounds came from the back of the house.

"They're probably in the family room," Alex said, and led the way. They passed a cream and gold dining room, which held a large table, already set.

At the end of the hall was a bright kitchen. Two women stood by the stove, one of them stirring something. Spicy smells reached out toward Marisol. Beyond the kitchen was the family room, where a TV was on and people watched a ballgame.

"Hi everyone," Alex said.

"Alejandro!" One of the women at the stove whirled around. She was attractive, with dark hair pulled back into a bun. This must be Alex's mother, Marisol thought. He looked a lot like her, although she was shorter.

"Mother, this is Marisol Acevedo," he introduced her. "Marisol, my mom."

"It's nice to meet you," Marisol said as the older woman wiped her hands on an apron and approached. She wore a black skirt and black and purple print top, and Marisol wondered if she was dressed up enough.

"Welcome," Alex's mother said with a small smile. She seemed to be studying Marisol.

"Aunt Teresa, this is Marisol," Alex was continuing.

His aunt, a short woman with snow-white hair, smiled serenely as she came over to meet Marisol. She wore a blue flowered dress. "How nice that you could come to dinner," she said, her tone friendly.

"Alex?" The man who appeared at the doorway to the family room must be Alex's father. With a headful of dark hair shot with gray, Marisol could see Alex resembled him too, though he looked more like his mother.

Alex introduced her to his father, Ricardo. Ricardo pumped her hand enthusiastically. "It's a pleasure to meet you," he said.

Marisol offered to help with the meal, but Mrs. Lares told her to sit and relax.

As she left the kitchen, Marisol heard Teresa whisper to Mrs. Lares in Italian.

"She's a nice girl. And very pretty."

She shouldn't have been surprised that they knew Italian. It wasn't that hard to learn another of the romance languages if you knew one already, like Spanish or French or Portuguese. Marisol had taken Italian in college, since she was fluent in Spanish and wanted to try a different language. She loved the way the language sounded too, and used to practice with her closest friend from college, Roseanna, who was Italian.

Alex's aunt probably knew she'd understand Spanish, and had spoken in Italian, thinking she wouldn't know exactly what was said, despite many similarities in the language.

Now she thought they'd be embarrassed if they knew she had heard—and understood—the whispers.

Alex guided Marisol into the family room, where she met Juan Carlos, Maria, and their son, Matthew, a sandy-haired toddler. Alex's brother and sister-in-law were dressed more casually than the older adults, Marisol observed.

"Acevedo . . ." Maria was saying. She wore jeans and a red and white maternity top, and looked like she must be about midway through her pregnancy. "I grew up in Dover—that's where you're from, right? I know several Acevedos."

They chatted, discovering that Marisol's cousin Rafael had graduated with Maria.

Alex's father sat in a chair while the younger Lares played on the floor with their son. Marisol perched on the leather couch, and Alex sat beside her, close.

People immediately began to pepper her with questions.

"So you teach salsa?" "When did you learn?" "How do you like being a librarian?" were only a few that were thrown her way.

At least Alex's family, though curious, was friendly.

She answered all of them, and played with Matthew when he began handing her blocks.

"Dinner is ready," Mrs. Lares announced.

Marisol felt Alex's hand at her elbow, and he steered her toward the dining room. His father sat at one end of the table, and she found herself seated on his left, with Alex on her other side. Alex's mother sat at the opposite end, nearest to the kitchen.

Fortunately the house was cool because there were plenty of hot dishes set out. Marisol enjoyed cooking, and had studied enough cookbooks at the library to know that meat was popular in Argentinian dishes. Mr. Lares told her he had grilled the steaks that were heaped on a platter, after they had marinated overnight in his wife's special sauce.

There was also salad, a heaping bowl of rice, grilled corn, a mixed vegetable dish, and fried fish.

"Did you catch the fish yourself?" Marisol asked as they began to pass the serving bowls around.

Mr. Lares shook his head. "I do some fishing, but no, these came straight from the grocery."

"Here, try the garlic bread," Aunt Teresa said, passing it to Alex, but speaking to Marisol. She must have seen Marisol's surprise. "We love garlic bread," she added. "I made it. You know, in Buenos Aires, there is a large Italian population. We have many Italian friends there and we all like Italian food."

Ahh. Now Marisol understood their fluency in Italian. "I love Italian food also," she said, and helped herself to some bread before passing it to Alex's father. She was tempted to say it in Italian, but stopped herself.

She put a little of everything on her plate, and still it overflowed. She tried some of the fried flounder. "This is delicious," she said to Alex's mother. "How did you make it?"

"I dredge the fish in flour mixed with a little paprika, salt, and pepper . . . ," she began.

Mrs. Lares had been regarding her cautiously, Marisol feared. But as they began to chat about recipes, she thought the older woman was relaxing.

"And I crush garlic for the meat marinade, it's so much better than using garlic powder . . . ," she continued.

The food was delicious. Their cooking conversation continued for a few minutes, and then Mrs. Lares said, "Your Spanish is quite good, you know."

Marisol looked at her, startled. She hadn't thought about it, but the last few minutes they had been conversing in Spanish. Mrs. Lares spoke in a slightly more formal way than most of the people Marisol knew. This must be why Alex did, she thought.

"Mother . . ." Alex's tone held a warning note.

Mrs. Lares smiled suddenly. "It is all right, Alex." She addressed Marisol. "Everyone knows that I think that only those from Spain and South America speak the best Spanish. But you speak quite well, Marisol."

"Thank you," Marisol murmured. She felt as if she was in high school and had just passed a test—barely. Noticing the frown on Alex's face, she decided to divert the topic slightly. "Do you speak many languages in your store?" she asked Alex's father.

"Yes, it has been convenient to know several. I speak English, Italian, and Portuguese, as well as Spanish," Mr. Lares said. "Juan Carlos does too."

"That's great," Marisol said. She turned to Alex. "Do you also?"

"I actually had to speak Portuguese to a patient from Brazil who came in this week," he said. "My Portuguese and Italian are passable but not great. I took German in high school and Japanese in college."

"Japanese!" Marisol was impressed. "That is a very difficult language. Have you been able to use it?"

"Only at Japanese restaurants," he said, and everyone laughed.

The rest of the dinner went more smoothly, and Marisol hoped that Alex's family liked her. His mother, at least, seemed warmer than when she'd first come in.

And Aunt Teresa was interesting, telling tales of life when she was a young girl, and some stories about Alex and Juan Carlos when they were small.

"Everyone in high school has heard of Alex," Marisol told his family. "They still talk about his reading the encyclopedia."

Alex shrugged, but she noticed his parents smiled widely.

"And going to Yale," she added.

Alex was beginning to look embarrassed, though she suspected his parents liked hearing about their son's excellent reputation.

Everyone seemed to be finished. Juan Carlos had Matthew on his lap now, playing with some spoons, since he'd gotten restless. When Alex's mother and aunt got up to clear the dishes, Marisol followed, bringing in several plates.

"You're a guest, you shouldn't be helping," Mrs. Lares protested.

"No, of course I'll help," Marisol said. Maria had followed with a serving bowl, walking slowly.

Alex's father had gone into the family room and was playing with his grandson now. When Marisol turned to get more dishes, she bumped into Alex, who was carrying a serving platter with very little meat left.

She was glad to see that in his family, the men—at least he and Juan Carlos—were helping to clean up. She knew it frustrated her mother that her father didn't help, and neither did her uncles.

Alex's eyes met hers. She smiled. To her surprise, he winked at her.

Warmth flowed through her, to every limb.

"Come now, we should let the young people relax," Aunt Teresa said. "Alex, why don't you show Marisol the garden?"

"As soon as we're done," he replied, balancing several plates together.

Marisol brought the glasses she held over to his mother, who was filling the dishwasher. The stainless steel appliances in the kitchen gleamed, and Marisol surmised that with Mr. Lares in the appliance and furniture business, everything was state of the art.

"Go ahead, I'll finish up," Maria told them. "Go enjoy the garden." She smiled at Marisol.

Alex led the way outside into the backyard. Despite some shady trees, the air was warm. Beautiful flowers and bushes, nicely trimmed, lined a path that led to a small fountain with a statue of Mary.

"It's very peaceful," Marisol said.

"Yes." He stared at the fountain. Water splashed musically, and a small gray bird flew over to perch on the edge.

"I hope your family likes me," Marisol said.

He seemed surprised, and turned to face her. "Why wouldn't they? Oh—you mean my mother testing your Spanish?" He chuckled. "She does that with everyone she meets. Her pet theory is that no one but those from South America and Spain speak correct Spanish. And she believes the way you speak reflects your intelligence, character, and social class. Something left over from her upbringing, I guess, in parochial schools."

"Oh." Marisol didn't want to make too big a deal about it, but she hoped she'd gotten Mrs. Lares' approval.

"Anyway, I'm sure you don't have to worry. Who wouldn't like you?" he asked.

Marisol gazed up at Alex. Suddenly the garden seemed hushed, waiting.

He gently stroked his finger down her cheek. "Who wouldn't like you?" he repeated. This time it was a whisper.

"I . . ." Her voice faltered. *As long as you like me,* she wanted to say. Instead, she swallowed, her breath unsteady.

"Everyone likes you," he said, "especially . . . me."

Without thinking, Marisol reached up and clasped his hand in hers. They stood staring at each other, the humming of insects and birds and the splash of the fountain creating quiet background music so that it seemed the two of them stood in an enchanted garden.

Alex's eyes hadn't left hers. He opened his mouth, as if he was about to say something—

Marisol heard a noise, and then, "Alejandro! Marisol!" It was Mr. Lares' voice from the sliding glass door.

He didn't seem to realize he had interrupted their reverie. He continued, "Why don't you show us how you do the salsa?"

Alex stepped back, the intimate moment broken.

At Marisol's questioning look, he shook his head slightly. Turning to his father, he answered, "After I have a few more lessons."

Clunk! The soccer ball came at Alex with speed. He ran forward and kicked it to the side. Pablo ran but couldn't get there in time, and it rolled away.

Alex was breathing heavily. The soccer practice his cousin had suggested was turning into a real workout. In high school Alex, who was a year older, had been better on defense, where Pablo's strength was offense. Tonight Pablo was playing strongly, kicking fiercely, as if he was driven.

It had been his suggestion that they meet at Alex's condo complex when he called at lunchtime. There were parklike grounds and areas for kids—and adults—to play, and they had often kicked the ball around there. Right now, the sky was overcast and the wind had picked up, and on this early Monday evening, only the two of them and a couple playing tennis in the court nearby were outside.

"Let's take a break," Pablo suggested.

They walked over to a bench where they'd left their

water bottles and Alex drank the refreshing water. Pablo's aggressive playing made him suspect that something was bothering his cousin. Dropping to the seat, he waited for him to say what was on his mind.

Pablo drank quickly, then wiped his face with a towel and sat beside Alex.

Alex raised his eyebrows, and Pablo sighed. "I guess you can see that—I've got something on my mind."

"Either that or the devil is chasing you," Alex said, reaching for his own towel. "Want to talk?"

"Yeah." He sat back, looking suddenly beat.

Alex tried to appear relaxed, but inside he felt tense. Was Pablo going to bring up Celia?

But his cousin surprised him. "It's Irena," he said abruptly.

"Irena?" Alex asked. "What about her?"

"Yeah." Pablo leaned forward, wiping his face again with the towel. "I'm having some second thoughts about her. About marrying her."

"Oh." Alex was unsure what to say. "How long has this been going on?"

Pablo turned to him, a sardonic expression on his face. "Almost since we got engaged last fall."

This was news to Alex. "I had no idea," Alex said. "Do you love her?"

"That's just it . . . I thought I did when we got engaged, but . . . then a lot of little things began to happen. This big wedding, for one. It's driving me crazy. Not that I don't understand she wants it and all, I guess most women do, but—she wants to control everything about it and our marriage. And—me. She wants to control me. And it's getting worse," he added glumly. "First it's, 'We have to go here, Pablo,' or 'We have to go there.' Then it's, 'We have to do this; we have to do that.' Now she wants to decide where we're going to live. She isn't sure she likes my house. And she doesn't like my taste in furniture, so she's going to shop for furniture alone."

"Have you told her how you felt?" Alex asked.

"I've tried. She doesn't want to listen. It didn't bother me so much at first, but then . . . it's getting worse. I didn't mind her insisting on the salsa class, although insisting you go too was a little much. But now she's managing all our social events—" He stopped. "Have you noticed it?"

Alex sighed. "I have. And I didn't want to say anything, because I thought you were happy. But yes, Irena is very controlling." He tried to temper his comments with a calm tone. "I don't like to see her bossing you around so much."

"Ahh . . . so others have noticed." At Alex's nod, Pablo frowned. "I don't know what to do."

"Well, *amigo,* you better make up your mind soon. In less than two months you're supposed to walk down the aisle with her—and then there's no turning back," Alex reminded Pablo. "You know our families don't approve of divorce."

Pablo sighed loudly. "I know . . . and yet, I do care for her. I'm just not sure it's love. And on top of that—" He stopped and looked away toward the couple playing tennis, lobbing the ball at a steady rate.

"On top of that . . . ?" Alex asked quietly, having a feeling he knew what was coming.

"On top of that, I seem to have an—an infatuation for someone I met recently." He turned and faced Alex.

"If you loved Irena, would you really be infatuated with someone else?" Alex asked.

Pablo sat back, staring at Alex. Alex had a feeling his cousin hadn't thought about that.

"I don't know," Pablo drawled. "I mean, I could love Irena and still want to kiss someone else, can't I?"

"I don't know," Alex said. "If you love someone it's normal to notice an attractive woman—but to want to kiss her? I just don't know."

"That's because you're all wrapped up with Marisol," his cousin said. "She's beautiful—really hot looking—and she's nice too."

Alex felt a sudden sick feeling in his stomach. "You have a crush on her?"

Pablo shook his head, not meeting Alex's eyes. "No, not her." A bird landed near their feet, twittering.

Alex could breathe again. "On Celia?" he asked, his voice low.

"How did you know?" Pablo raised his eyebrows.

Seeing Pablo's surprise, he admitted, "I saw you kissing her at the carnival."

Pablo muttered something.

"So did Marisol," Alex continued. "But we're not going to say anything to Irena, if you're worried about that."

Pablo slapped his towel against his thigh. "I just

couldn't help it. We were laughing together, and she's so lovely and sincere and, before I knew it, my arms were around her and I was kissing her."

Alex leaned back. "What do you think that means?"

"That I better straighten this out before I get married," Pablo said grimly. "I just don't know—I mean, I hardly know Celia, but I keep thinking about her—"

Just as he, Alex, couldn't stop thinking about Marisol. But at least he wasn't in a relationship with someone else.

"I think," Alex told his cousin, "that you have to consider whether you want to spend your life with Irena. If you do, you better stop things with Celia before they go any further. If you don't want to continue with Irena, then you have to tell her. And then you have to decide if you want to explore this attraction to Celia."

Pablo stared at him. "You're right, doc." He flashed him a smile.

"Hey, how about we get cleaned up, then grab a bite to eat?" Alex suggested. He had gulped down a sandwich for dinner, but he knew he'd be hungry again soon. "Tomorrow's my day off. We can watch a DVD, get your mind off things for a while. You'll make a better decision if your head is clear," he finished.

"I knew talking to you would help me get my head on straight," Pablo said. "Okay, let's go. And . . . thanks."

As they walked back to Alex's condo, Pablo said casually, "So I hear you brought Marisol home to meet the folks. What's going on with you two?"

"I don't know."

"Hey, you listened to me . . . I can listen to your problems too," Pablo said.

"I keep thinking it was a mistake to bring her to meet the family," Alex said. "I mean, I'm very attracted to her . . . and it's not just that she's beautiful. She is really a warm person, vivacious and fun to be with. But . . ."

"But . . . ?" Pablo probed as wind gusted suddenly, cooling Alex's warm face.

He glanced at the sky. The clouds that had been threatening for the last few hours seemed to have lowered. They were going to have a storm later.

"I just don't know . . . I really don't want to get too involved," Alex said.

"Because of your experience with Juanita?"

Alex turned to look at his cousin. Pablo knew the complete story of his breakup with Juanita. The real version, not the short one he usually told people.

"I don't know," he began.

"Look, you shouldn't let one bad experience sour you on love, man." Pablo met his look.

"I'll think about it," Alex promised.

But when he thought of the heartache he'd felt after his split with Juanita, he knew it would be difficult to get involved with someone again. Why should he risk his heart?

Chapter Six

Marisol stretched out on her bed, a new romance novel in her hands.

On the other side of the long room, Christa was silent, studying for her history final. The hum of the air conditioner provided the only sound.

Marisol opened the book but, as had happened almost continually today, her mind went back to Alex.

She knew she was falling for him. And she was scared.

Not because she thought he didn't care for her. No— her women's intuition told her he liked her, a lot.

But it also told her that he was hesitant, and might not want to take their relationship to the next level.

And that scared her.

She'd already had one instance of almost-heartbreak, with Luis. She knew she had been smart to call off that relationship before she got even more involved. Mutual friends had told her recently that Luis had been dating the same woman for almost three years, and that Luis still refused to get married, and the woman was extremely upset.

You were smart to avoid that situation, Marisol told herself for the hundredth time.

Should she avoid a similar situation with Alex too?

A sudden drumming on the roof startled Marisol, breaking her train of thought. The rain that had threatened for several hours had arrived.

She sighed. She had to stop thinking about Alex.

She got up and lit a white jar candle on her dresser, enjoying the soothing vanilla scent, and then opened her book. Reading a good book always helped get her mind off her troubles. She eagerly immersed herself in the sparkling balls and exciting intrigues of regency England.

She tried to think about the book when she turned off the light and climbed into bed several hours later. Yet it was Alex's handsome face she pictured as she imagined the hero of the romance . . .

Marisol watched as the room began to fill up with students. The weather outside was warm and muggy, and despite the air-conditioning, the atmosphere seemed heavy. Rain had threatened again for most of the day, and thunderstorms were predicted for later. Maybe that was why the air seemed thick with warning.

Celia had been quite subdued when they first entered the studio. Marisol couldn't help wondering how she and Pablo were going to react to each other. And what about Irena? Plus she suspected Sondra would be upset if their class was the cause of a broken engagement.

"How's your foot?" Marisol asked her friend.

"Okay, really. I just have to be careful," Celia said. "I've tried to keep my weight off of it the last couple of days. I'll be all right."

Anne and Dominick wandered into the room, arms around each other. At least they look happy, Marisol thought.

She made sure there was plenty of water and lemonade ready. Turning from the table, she saw Irena and Pablo enter the room.

"Oh, let's go talk to Anne and Dominick," Irena was saying, and almost dragged Pablo over to the other couple.

Marisol glanced at Celia.

Celia was watching Pablo. And her expression made Marisol's stomach tighten with anxiety.

She really cares for him, Marisol thought. Celia looked . . . lovelorn.

Marisol started over toward her friend. Celia suddenly straightened and met Marisol's look. She gave her a small smile.

Fortunately, Marisol didn't think that Irena or Pablo had noticed anything. But would Celia's expressions give away her feelings toward Pablo later on?

She reached her friend's side. "Be careful," she whispered.

Celia nodded. Then something caught her eye, and

she whispered back, "Look, Marisol, at Shannon and Xavier."

Marisol pivoted, seeing Shannon and Xavier as they walked into the room. They were laughing, their gazes locked on each other.

Marisol took a quick breath. "I think we're seeing a real romance there."

"*Sí,*" Celia responded, her expression touched with wistfulness. Then she seemed to mentally shake herself. "And not just them, either." She gave Marisol a sideways look and a smile.

Marisol flushed.

Alex was entering the room. She couldn't help it, her heart immediately picked up its pace.

He looked around, and his eyes met hers.

He smiled.

And Marisol, smiling back, felt her heart dance.

Sondra was calling the class to order, and Marisol and Celia took their places at the head of the room so they could begin reviewing last week's steps.

The class usually sped by for Marisol. But tonight's was an exception. Even her students seemed tense, and made one mistake after another.

She tried to keep an eye on Irena and Pablo. Irena seemed absolutely fine, and Marisol concluded that she had no idea about what had happened between Pablo and Celia. Irena continued to boss people, directing Pablo where they should stand, and later, when they had switched partners, Marisol heard Irena correcting Leo's steps.

She's acting like she's the teacher, Marisol thought. She was going to say something, then decided to let it go. Leo could speak up if he wanted to.

Alex seemed to be in a somber mood, she observed, as he danced first with Stella, the middle-aged woman, and then with Shannon. It was hard not to keep looking over at him, and she had to force herself to keep her mind on her work.

Celia kept her eyes conspicuously off of Pablo. But once Marisol noticed him gazing after her.

She hoped Irena hadn't noticed. Not wanting to draw attention to Pablo or Celia with her own actions, Marisol purposefully didn't look at Irena.

Sondra called for the first break, and with relief Marisol went to get a drink of cool water.

Irena was standing near the cooler, speaking animatedly to Leo, Xavier, and Shannon. Pablo had stepped back, and Marisol sensed he was waiting for Celia to get close.

Marisol quickly stepped over, not wanting any suspicions to enter Irena's mind, and began talking to Pablo, hoping to distract him.

And hoping his cousin would join them.

"How are you, Marisol?" Pablo asked. "I hear you met some of the family."

"Yes, and they're very nice," she responded.

"Did my aunt test your Spanish?" Pablo asked with a smile.

Marisol returned the smile. "Yes, she did. I *think* I passed," she said.

"With flying colors," Alex said, coming up behind her. "Although it's kind of ridiculous. You don't have to impress my family," he added, looking directly at Marisol.

Her heart had started beating hard the moment she felt him behind her. "Oh. Well, I want to make a good impression," she said, keeping her voice light.

"You do." He smiled, but it didn't quite reach his eyes.

What was wrong? She wondered. He seemed . . . kind of withdrawn, or something. Was he thinking about Pablo and Celia?

"Did you have a rough day at the hospital?" she asked with a sympathetic smile.

Alex shook his head. "I had today off."

Before she could think of anything else to say, she heard Irena's voice. "Well, Marisol, what do you think? It seems I've made a match with Shannon and Xavier." She nodded her head toward the couple, who were beside the lemonade cooler, their heads bent together, speaking softly. Irena's voice held a smug note.

"They do seem to be getting along," Marisol observed.

Irena frowned suddenly. "Now where is Leo?"

Uh-oh. No way was Marisol going to have Irena try to maneuver Leo over toward herself. Besides, didn't Irena realize she had a thing for Alex? Unless Irena thought Alex didn't care for her.

Marisol edged away. "I have to ask Sondra something," she said, and left the group quickly.

She managed to make up a question for Sondra, and then it was time to get back to dancing.

True to her word, Sondra had brought her husband, and they demonstrated an entire number with dramatic flourishes that were skilled and impressive as well as hot and romantic. The class applauded loudly when they finished.

"Thank you, thank you," Sondra and her husband said.

"Think we'll be able to do that?" Dominick teased, elbowing Anne.

"It is possible, if you practice for years, as we do," Sondra said, smiling. Turning to the class, she had them line up, and began teaching another variation, barely out of breath.

Marisol and Celia demonstrated, although Celia reminded everyone she had to be careful with her foot. The class lined up and repeated the steps several times. And then Sondra put on music and they practiced some more.

When they broke into couples, Marisol found herself dancing at first with the talkative woman. Sondra must have spoken to her, because she had toned down considerably. Marisol praised her as she caught on to the steps.

Next she was paired with Xavier, who had natural rhythm and danced easily. She enjoyed their few minutes together. He really was a nice guy, and she could see why Shannon liked him.

It was soon time for their next break, and everyone again gravitated toward the coolers.

"It looks like we're going to have quite a storm," Stella observed, glancing out the window. "I hope it holds off until we leave."

"We're supposed to get thunderstorms all night," Celia volunteered, staring out at the dark gray clouds. It wasn't sunset yet, but it was so dark, it looked almost like night-time. Catching Marisol's eye, she lowered her voice. "It's dark and gloomy . . . just the way my life is going."

"Oh, Celia." Marisol gave her friend's arm a squeeze. Celia continued to look out the window. Marisol was afraid she could see heartache in her friend's eyes.

She really did care about Pablo. What a mess!

"Marisol?" Anne had come up behind her. "I have a question . . ."

Anne needed help, and they practiced together. Then they went to get cold water. As she sipped the refreshing drink, Marisol spotted Pablo and Alex, talking quietly.

Talking about what, she wondered?

Sondra was clapping her hands, and they lined up to practice what they had just been taught. Marisol stayed near Anne, helping her till she was sure Anne had the hang of it.

"Thanks." Anne flashed her a smile.

When Sondra had half the class move three places to the right, Marisol found herself facing Irena.

She prayed that Irena wouldn't guess that Celia had feelings for Pablo. Brightly she asked Irena, "Shall we dance?"

"This is getting harder," Irena admitted. "I think I'll stick to the basic variations after this class!"

"Oh, but it will be fun to salsa at your wedding," Marisol said.

Irena nodded. "If I don't step on anyone's feet."

"You're doing fine," Marisol told her, guiding her through the steps. Irena was doing well.

When they switched partners again, she suddenly found herself with Alex.

Marisol's mouth went dry. Her senses seemed to leap to attention so that she was acutely aware of the handsome man in front of her, the shadowy growth on his face, the spicy cologne that was faint yet recognizable, and the serious expression in his eyes. She forced herself to smile and took his hand, and they stood in the correct position til the music began

"You dance divinely," he said quietly as they moved through the motions of the dance.

"Thank you," she murmured. She smiled up at him again. There was no answering smile on his face, just a pensive look that bothered Marisol. What was he thinking about?

A determined look crept over his features, and she realized he was concentrating on the steps. "You're doing fine," she praised.

"It's not easy," he replied, not complaining, just stating a fact. She could see that for him it wasn't easy.

"Relax, and feel the rhythm of the music," she urged.

He didn't look relaxed, though, and she suspected it wasn't only because he was concentrating on the dance.

It was the first time she had felt uncomfortable dancing with Alex. It was as if a wall surrounded him, a wall she couldn't penetrate with her smile. She could see him perfectly, but something stood between them. Was he worried about Pablo and Irena? she speculated.

"Very good," Sondra said suddenly. She was moving from one couple to another. She smiled at Alex. "Just relax, Dr. Lares. This is not surgery. A mistake is not fatal."

Alex smiled at that, and Marisol was grateful that Sondra's quip had lightened the mood.

When the dance ended, Sondra instructed them to change partners again. Marisol faced Stella, and next to them were Irena and Pablo.

As the music started, Marisol observed Irena saying something to Pablo. He was frowning, and Irena didn't look too happy, either.

She hoped it had nothing to do with Celia!

Class ended a little while later. For once people didn't linger. Someone announced that it was lightning and it looked like the rain was imminent, and people began to hurry out. As she cleaned up, Marisol saw Xavier put his arm around Shannon and hold her close as they exited together.

Irena and Pablo appeared to be arguing, though they were too far away for Marisol to hear the words. She swallowed, working more quickly. She'd left her umbrella in the car and didn't want to be caught in a downpour.

As they put away the cold drinks and straightened up, she glanced around for Alex, but he seemed to have disappeared.

Sondra waved at Celia and Marisol. "My husband will help me lock up. You two go ahead, before the rain comes."

Thanking her, Marisol and Celia scooted outside.

"Oh no," Celia said.

The clouds had opened up and the rain was just starting to stream down. Thunder rumbled.

"I'll walk you to your cars."

Alex's voice, from just outside the door, startled Marisol. She turned to find him standing with a large umbrella. Waiting for them—for her!

"Thank you!" she said.

She and Celia huddled under Alex's large black umbrella. The hope that she'd get a word in with Alex faded away when she realized that Celia's car was farther away than her own. They paused by her car, and Marisol fished in her purse for her keys. "Thanks again," she said, as Alex held the umbrella so that she could slide into her car while he and Celia remained dry.

"No problem," he said.

He and Celia backed away and Marisol shut her door before she got drenched. She started the car and watched as he led Celia to her car, and she got in. Then Alex turned and walked back to his car.

Her heart sank. It looked like Alex was just being gentlemanly, not like he had waited to speak to her. She put her windshield wipers on full force and flicked on the car lights and radio.

Well, he had her cell number and her number at home. He could always call her.

Celia was already pulling out of her parking space. Marisol followed her slowly, getting ready to leave the parking lot.

As she glanced in the rearview mirror, she saw Alex standing in the rain, under his umbrella, beside his car. Making no move to get in, just staring after her.

It was too dark and he was too far away for her to see his expression. But as he stood in the rain, he looked lonely.

Or was that simply her overactive imagination?

She sighed, and looking both ways at the rain-filled street, pulled out of the parking lot and headed home.

"Gracias, señorita," the young mother said, picking up the books Marisol had helped her select.

"De nada," Marisol responded, smiling.

The woman, Mrs. Alvarez, had come in many times, looking for simple books she could read to her young son, and books her older son could enjoy too. Marisol was always glad to help. Though Mrs. Alvarez could speak a little English, she was much more comfortable conversing in Spanish with Marisol.

Her younger son, who was about two, was a handful and was constantly trying to climb on the bookcases. Just ten minutes earlier Marisol had had to remind Mrs. Alvarez to keep a close watch on him.

"We don't want him to get hurt," she'd said gently.

Mrs. Alvarez turned to Joyce, and proceeded to check out the books. Marisol went to help another customer, a mother who had questions about the local school's upcoming summer reading project. As she strode toward the shelves containing the required books, she had to walk through a patch of the morning sunshine. Despite the air-conditioning in the library, this spot was hot and she knew the day was going to be a warm one.

"The fourth-grade selections are right here," Marisol began, when a sudden cry interrupted her.

She turned to see little Ray Alvarez on the floor. Mrs. Alvarez began screaming. "*Mi hijo! Mi hijo!*"

"Excuse me," she said to the other mother, and hurried to the little boy.

He was crying and screaming, and bleeding from his forehead.

Another mother had come forward. "I saw him standing on a chair, and he fell and hit his head on the edge of the bookcase," she told Marisol.

Marisol dropped to her knees. "It's all right," she said in her most soothing voice.

But it wasn't. His forehead was bleeding a lot, and she could see a nasty-looking gash there.

"Call 9-1-1!" she called to Joyce. She turned toward Mrs. Alvarez. In Spanish she said, "We're calling 9-1-1. Try to calm him, and I'll get some cold water."

She sprang up, afraid that the little boy's mother needed as much calming as he did. Her shrieks weren't helping. She ran into the back room, and tearing some paper towels off a roll, soaked them in cold water. Squeezing them out slightly, she ran back.

The boy was still screaming, and Mrs. Alvarez was trying to hold him but she was crying too, still moaning "My son!" in Spanish.

"Here, let me," Marisol said, and kneeling next to her, tried to apply the cold compress to the boy.

He swatted at her, screaming louder.

"The emergency squad is coming," Joyce said over his cries.

The other mother who had witnessed the accident was trying to help, but the little boy was now thrashing his legs as he screamed. Marisol was afraid he was going to kick his mother in the ribs.

"Shh, it will be all right," she said, trying to calm him and get the cold paper towel on his forehead to stop the bleeding.

She succeeded in getting it plastered to his bleeding forehead, but only for a minute or two before he began pushing at it, and her. Thankfully she heard the sound of a siren only two minutes later.

The emergency squad members calmly entered the room, and quickly assessed the situation. "Looks like he'll need stitches," said an older woman.

Marisol translated for his crying mother. The volunteers from the squad brought in a stretcher. "We'll have to strap him down so he doesn't hurt himself," the woman said to Mrs. Alvarez, who was trying to hold her kicking child. "Or else you'll have to hold him."

Marisol rapidly translated. Mrs. Alvarez, weeping, lifted her screaming son and went with the emergency personnel toward the ambulance.

Turning, Mrs. Alvarez cried out to Marisol in Spanish, "Please come with me!"

A tall man said, "You can follow us in your car. If she needs a translator, I can speak a little Spanish. *Yo hablo un poco español*," he told Mrs. Alvarez.

"No, no, I want you!" she cried in Spanish, her tearful face imploring Marisol.

The director of the library, Mrs. Woods, had been standing nearby for several minutes, trying to help. "You go," she urged Marisol.

"I'll follow the ambulance in my car," Marisol promised the distraught mother.

As soon as they took Mrs. Alvarez and her son outside, she raced to get her purse and keys, then out to her car. She was ready as soon as they were and followed the ambulance out of the parking lot, down the road, and onto the main highway.

She was driving for a few minutes when she realized they were headed to the hospital where Alex worked.

Would he be on duty?

She followed the ambulance until it pulled into the ambulance entry area. Driving into the emergency room parking lot, she parked and hurried into the hospital.

The strong antiseptic smell greeted her. She could hear little Ray screaming his head off and followed the sound to an emergency examining room.

A security guard stepped in front of her. "You can't go in there."

"I'm translating for my friend," she told him.

"Señorita Acevedo!" Mrs. Alvarez called, poking her head out of the examining area.

She was almost as hysterical as her son. Marisol said to her soothingly, in Spanish, "It's all right. They'll take care of your little one. Please, calm yourself, *señora*. It will be better for him if you are calm."

A receptionist was trying to get information from the distraught woman. Mrs. Alvarez took a breath, and Marisol could see she was attempting to calm herself down. Quickly, Marisol explained what had happened. The receptionist asked a couple of questions, and Marisol translated for Mrs. Alvarez and gave her answers while a nurse tried to look at Ray's wound.

A powerful, masculine yet calm voice broke through the chaos. "Let's see your face, buddy, and we'll make you feel better," Alex said in Spanish.

Relief engulfed Marisol. She saw it on Mrs. Alvarez's face as well. Here was a doctor who spoke Spanish and could take care of the little boy.

He smiled at little Ray and gently held his head as he examined the wound. "It's all right, you'll be better soon," he told him. "I'm going to give you something to make it feel better." Without looking at the nurse he began giving quiet orders, and gave Ray an oral sedative. Finally he glanced up at Mrs. Alvarez. "It's a simple laceration," he said. "He'll need stitches, but this isn't as bad as it looks."

"Will he be all right?" she asked.

"Yes, he'll be fine," he answered in the same soothing voice. "Try to remain calm, it will make him feel better. As soon as he is sedated, I'll do the stitches."

Mrs. Alvarez sucked in her breath. "I will try, doctor." She glanced at Marisol.

For the first time, Alex looked beyond Mrs. Alvarez and met Marisol's eyes.

His eyes widened as he registered who was with Mrs. Alvarez, but he said nothing. Turning back to the boy, who was beginning to quiet down, he kept speaking in his professional, soothing tone.

A nurse came in and Alex disappeared, returning fifteen minutes later. Ray had stopped sobbing and was looking sleepy by then. Alex instructed Mrs. Alvarez to stand where her son could see her, and to talk soothingly to him as the nurse held him and he stitched him up. She did, but she held Marisol's hand in a death grip.

Marisol remained silent. She couldn't help admiring the calm and efficient way Alex worked, and the kindness he showed the little boy while getting his job done.

Before she knew it he was finished, and the nurse was taking away the instruments. The little boy had a bandage on his forehead, and Alex spoke quietly to him before turning to his mother with some instructions.

"And there is some information the receptionist needs," he added.

"*Sí*," Mrs. Alvarez said. She glanced at Marisol. "Can you help me?"

"Of course," Marisol said.

"You'll feel better now, Ray," Alex said to the little boy. Crouching down so that they were eye to eye, he finished, "You go home and watch some cartoons for the afternoon, yes? No more rough play today."

The little boy clutched his mother's hand. "*Sí.*"

Alex's eyes met Marisol's.

At that exact moment, Marisol felt her heart tumbling, sliding, splashing into a pool of emotion.

Love.

She was in love with Alex!

It felt wonderful!

Chapter Seven

It felt awful.

Marisol dragged herself to her car, suddenly weary. She had waited with Mrs. Alvarez after helping her answer standard questions for the hospital forms. She'd offered to drive them home, since Mrs. Alvarez's husband was working today all the way in Jersey City. But Mrs. Alvarez insisted she had already done enough, and called her brother, who lived in Dover. He'd just arrived to pick them up.

The burst of excitement Marisol had first felt when she realized she was in love with Alex had been glorious. She was in love! Finally, after all these years, she knew what the feeling was! To love and care for another human being—to want to be with him all the time—to feel not only an intense attraction, but a longing to be in his company, respect for him, a spiritual connection—all of these things were interconnected, and she felt them all for Alejandro Lares.

She had forced herself to push the feelings aside so she could help Mrs. Alvarez. She'd wanted to speak to Alex, but before she could open her mouth someone was calling, "Dr. Lares! Mrs. Carter is back from X-ray!" and he'd disappeared without a word.

Now she walked slowly through the midday heat to her parked car. The giddy excitement she'd felt had dwindled while she waited with Mrs. Alvarez, and was slowly being replaced with anxiety about discovering love.

What if Alex didn't feel the same?

What if he liked her, but didn't love her? Or he loved her, but didn't want a commitment—if he was like Luis? Or his family didn't care for her? Or—

"Marisol!"

The shout came from behind her. She whirled around to see Alex was striding toward her, his white lab coat flapping as he hurried forward.

Suddenly she felt wonderful again.

"I'm sorry I couldn't talk before," he said as he drew closer.

"It's all right," she reassured him. "I could see you were busy. You have life-and-death matters to take care of."

"Not today, fortunately," he told her, grinning suddenly. "But I'm working a lot of hours the next few days. The father of one of our doctors died suddenly, and he had to go up to Massachusetts for several days. So we're shorthanded."

"I understand," she said, trying not to appear as excited as she felt. Her heart was doing cartwheels inside her chest. She smiled at him. "If you just want to come over and hang out one evening, we can do that."

"Actually, Friday I don't have to work late. Want to see a movie?" he asked.

What a question. She'd be happy watching a cartoon with him!

"I'd love to. And . . . why don't you come early and have dinner?"

She saw Alex hesitate. Was he reluctant to spend time with her family?

"My grandmother would love to see you again," she added.

"Okay, but don't fuss," Alex said, grinning. "I'll eat anything."

Marisol had Friday off, so it would be easy enough to help make a nice dinner. But she agreed. "Okay." She'd try to think of something simple and delicious— maybe they would grill hamburgers on the deck, and she could make homemade potato salad . . .

"I better get back," Alex said. He hesitated, then stepped closer, and bent to kiss her swiftly on the lips. "You were a big help to your friend."

"She's someone who comes into the library often," Marisol said, hardly aware of the words coming from her mouth. Alex's kiss had been quick, but still sent warmth cascading down to her toes.

"I'll see you Friday," he said, starting to move back.

"Friday," she murmured. Then she shook herself

mentally. She had to get out of this kiss-induced haze of warmth and act like a normal person discussing dinner. "Six o'clock?"

"Fine." He smiled and then turned and strode back inside the hospital.

Marisol dreamily let herself back into the car. Friday. In two days she'd see him again.

And the feeling of being in love was once again wonderful.

She tried to keep it casual at dinnertime when she mentioned to her family that Alex was coming on Friday for supper.

"So he is coming here!" Her grandmother looked almost triumphant. "What should I cook?"

"What are you going to wear?" asked Christa.

Marisol bent her head, grinning. Her family was zany, but funny. Sometimes.

"Maybe my *paella,*" her grandmother continued.

"Friday! Oh, Pedro, we should have painted the living room and dining room last weekend," her mother moaned. "I told you not to put it off . . ."

"He's not coming here to look at the walls," Marisol's father stated. "He's coming to look at Marisol."

"But we want him to think our house looks nice," her mother countered. "And we were going to paint anyway."

"No, don't paint just because he's coming," Marisol said hastily. "The rooms look fine." Turning to Christa, she asked, "What do you think I should wear? We're going to the movies later."

"Oh, your short denim skirt for sure—or maybe the khaki skirt," Christa suggested.

"The room needs to be painted," her mother continued.

"He likes Italian food, yes? Maybe I'll make spaghetti," Grandma mused.

Marisol sighed. She should have known everyone would get totally excited.

"Look," she said, "he's just coming for a casual dinner. I thought we could grill something—and then we're going to the movies—"

"No, we should make something special for the doctor," *Mamita* said.

"He's probably not too interested in the food either," her father pointed out. "He just wants to see Marisol."

"And look us over." Her mother actually looked a little nervous.

"How about hamburgers and corn on the cob?" Marisol said, turning to her grandmother. "I'll make potato salad and Mom can make her garden salad—"

"And my homemade biscuits," *Mamita* finished.

"Yes, that would be great," Marisol said.

Really, they were making such a big deal about Alex eating here, you'd think they were getting married or something.

Marisol's thoughts came to a screeching halt.

Isn't that what she wanted? Deep inside?

Uh-oh. She hoped her family hadn't picked up on how serious her feelings were. Her feelings were too new, too exciting, too fragile to share with anyone just yet.

Except maybe Carina, and Celia.

Marisol tried to change the subject and told them about the little boy at the library and his injury.

As soon as they finished eating and she'd helped to clean up, she fed Pepé and volunteered to walk him. Grabbing her cell phone, she left the house. Everyone had big ears and at least outside she could speak to Carina without her family hearing everything.

She managed to fill Carina in on the events of the day—she'd already told her everything preceding that—as she and Pepé walked up the block and around the corner. Heading back, she listened to her friend's advice.

"You should try to make this a casual dinner . . . then Alex might be more relaxed," her friend said. "It sounds like he's a little uptight. Can you invite anyone else? Not your family. I mean, friends or neighbors or something. I'd suggest me, but I have a date."

They got sidetracked on that subject for a minute or two. Then, as Marisol approached her house, she had an idea.

"Maybe I can invite his cousin Pablo and his fiancée Irena!" she said. "With two more people there, the focus won't be so much on Alex. Carina, you're brilliant."

"No," her friend said, but she laughed. "It's a good idea, though. Everyone will be busy talking to them because your family doesn't already know them—they'll ask about the wedding and everything. That will get the focus off of Alex, and hopefully he'll feel more at ease. I think you should do it."

"I will!" Marisol declared. She paused to stare at a

house up the street from hers. A FOR SALE sign had been posted there sometime today.

She said good-bye and she and Pepé walked back to her house. After giving him a treat and checking to see he had plenty of water, Marisol went upstairs and looked up Irena's name and phone number on her class list.

Irena picked up on the first ring, and quickly accepted the invitation.

After giving her directions to her house, Marisol hung up, and stared at the phone.

A sudden, overwhelming guilt swamped her. What was she doing? One of her closest friends was in love with Pablo—and she was inviting him and his fiancée over for dinner. If Celia knew, she'd be hurt.

She'd been so concerned with making Alex feel at ease she hadn't thought about Celia and her crush—or maybe even her love—for Pablo. How could she do that to her friend?

Marisol stared at her hands, which were twisting her black and white skirt, crumpling the material, which felt so smooth against her skin.

She sighed. Well, it was too late now to change her mind. Irena had accepted—without consulting Pablo, which seemed typical for her—and that was that.

She hadn't told her family, either. Not that they would mind—they loved company, and she was sure they'd like the idea.

She'd have to explain what she'd done to Celia. And hope that Celia wouldn't be mad. She was just trying to make Alex feel comfortable.

Speaking of him, she'd better let him know about the extra guests too.

Knowing how many hours he was working this week, she wasn't surprised when she got his voice mail. She left him a brief message, ending with "I'll see you Friday!" in a tone that was more upbeat than the way she was feeling.

Sighing again, she changed to shorts and a T-shirt and went downstairs to let her family know about Irena and Pablo.

"Somebody just pulled up in front," Christa announced as she helped Marisol set the table.

Marisol glanced at the fence, straining to see the street from the deck. She hoped it was Alex.

It was a beautiful June evening. The heat wave of the last few days had diminished, and the air was warm but dry and delightful. A perfect evening to barbecue and eat outdoors on the deck.

"I'll get the door," Marisol volunteered. As she stepped into the kitchen, Pepé began barking at the front door.

Irena and Pablo had arrived, bringing a bottle of wine. Marisol introduced them to her parents, grandmother, and Christa. Almost immediately, her mother began asking them questions as she led them out to the deck.

Something is wrong, Marisol thought as she followed them. She could see tension in Pablo's expression, although he was acting friendly toward her parents. His posture was stiff and he hardly looked at Irena.

Irena, on the other hand, was talking more animatedly

than usual. She was describing the décor at the place where she'd planned the reception. But Marisol sensed that her enthusiasm was forced.

Had they had a fight just before coming here? she wondered.

Worse, had they had a fight about Celia?

"How long have you known each other?" Marisol's mom asked as they they took seats on the patio chairs. Her father opened up the wine and began pouring it into glasses.

"Not long," Pablo said. Irena shot him a look Marisol couldn't decipher.

"We knew each other two months when we got engaged," Irena said. "I knew a week after we met—at a party—that I was going to marry Pablo."

"She asked me, actually," Pablo said, in a tone bordering on resentful.

Everyone turned to look at him. Marisol saw her grandma's eyebrows shoot up, and even Christa looked surprised.

Irena shot him a dirty look. "Not exactly," she said. "We were talking about the future, and I said something, and he said something, and, well . . ."

Now Pablo looked annoyed. "You did ask, Irena."

"Women can do the asking today!" Christa piped up.

"Maybe in your generation," Papa said. Marisol sent her father a look. There was no sense making things worse. But her father seemed oblivious. "In my day, men did the asking."

Marisol wanted to groan.

Her mother spoke up suddenly. "Things are different with this generation, dear," she said amicably. She smiled at Irena, then Pablo, and Marisol sensed she was making an attempt to diffuse the situation.

"Women should do the asking more often," *Mamita* said staunchly. "My sister should have asked her suitor. It took him over a year to pop the question!"

Everyone laughed, and some of the tension eased out of the air.

Marisol's mother changed the subject. "So are you enjoying the salsa classes? Marisol said you wanted to learn for the wedding reception."

"Yes, we are," Pablo answered.

"Very much so," Irena said.

"Maybe you can demonstrate later!" *Mamita* urged.

The bell rang, and Pepé ran to the fence.

Marisol's heart jumped up. It must be Alex.

She was wrong. It was Manuel and his daughter and son-in-law. Marisol's mother had decided to invite them, too, after Marisol had told her she'd invited Irena and Pablo.

They'd brought wine too. Marisol greeted them and was leading the way to the kitchen door and the deck when the bell rang again.

Marisol carefully stepped around Pepé and Manuel's dog, Priscilla, who were happily scrambling around together.

When she opened the door, her heart flew into her throat.

Alex stood there. In a dark red polo shirt and black jeans, he looked wonderful.

Except that there was something in his expression . . . something that made her heart clutch.

Was it weariness? Or something else?

"C'mon in," she invited, holding the door open. She got a faint whiff of his masculine, spicy aftershave. "I guess this was a long week for you?"

"You're not kidding." She heard the note of fatigue in his voice. "And we lost a patient this morning."

"I'm sorry." Without thinking, she reached out and touched his cheek, gently. "That must be so hard. What happened?"

He reached up and gripped her hand, hard. "A man came in with a massive stroke. I tried, the whole team tried but, there was nothing we could do." She saw the sadness in his eyes. "He was only fifty-four."

"Fifty-four? How terrible."

He took a deep breath. "Thanks. Oh—" He let go of her hand, and with his other one he handed her a bouquet of colorful flowers. "For you, and your mother, and grandmother."

"Thank you!" Marisol said, sniffing the red roses, which were surrounded by daisies and white and yellow carnations. The roses smelled sweet and romantic. "You didn't have to do this." She fingered a velvety petal.

"It's nothing," he said, shrugging.

She preceded him out the back and onto the deck, where she introduced Alex to her neighbors.

She saw a flash of something in Pablo's eyes, and she got the distinct feeling that he was relieved to see Alex.

Manuel was asking about the salsa classes too.

"We can have a demonstration after dinner," Irena said.

Marisol could have sworn Pablo rolled his eyes.

Marisol's father asked who wanted hamburgers, hot dogs, and chicken, and began grilling while Marisol and her mother put out the salads.

Marisol was relieved when the conversation turned to soccer, and the men began debating the merits of their favorite teams.

At least her family was not asking Alex too many nosy questions. She relaxed, and tried to follow the ups and downs of the Brazilian team they were discussing.

When the food was ready everyone lined up by the side table and helped themselves. Manuel's daughter, Alberta, was asking Irena some questions about her honeymoon.

"I've always wanted to go to Las Vegas," Irena said. "It sounds so exciting! So we're going there."

Marisol glanced at Pablo. He was helping himself to her potato salad and acting as if he wasn't listening to Irena, but she noticed his mouth tighten.

"I've heard it's very lavish there," Marisol's mom said.

"And they have wonderful entertainment," *Mamita* added.

"I've never been there, but my sister said it's lots of fun," Alberta said.

The subject turned to traveling and places people wanted to see. Christa talked about how she'd like to see Stonehenge, and *Mamita* spoke about wanting to someday travel through Spain and Portugal. Marisol mentioned her desire to see the pyramids in Egypt.

"Mexico is fascinating," Alex spoke up. "Have you ever been there?" he asked Marisol.

She shook her head. "Outside of New Jersey and New York, I've visited Miami twice, Puerto Rico several times, and the Bahamas once."

"There are some beautiful areas and also some interesting ruins," Alex said. "And of course, Argentina is wonderful too."

Marisol's mom said that she was thinking that for their next anniversary, she and Marisol's dad might visit Jamaica.

"I'd like to go there too, sometime," Irena said.

They continued to speak about places they'd visited and ones they hoped to. While Irena seemed to have a whole list of places she intended to travel to, Pablo remained silent on the subject.

"What about you?" *Mamita* asked him suddenly.

Pablo shrugged. "Traveling can be fun. There's no place I'm very anxious to see, except maybe the Grand Canyon. I've always wanted to go there."

Marisol opened her mouth, then shut it abruptly. She'd been about to say she had a friend who'd always wanted to go there—then stopped herself in time. Celia was the one who wanted to see the Grand Canyon! And she didn't want to bring up her name, not to Pablo—or Irena.

Irena was frowning. "I didn't know that."

"You never asked." Pablo met her eyes.

Irena's lips thinned. "You never volunteered that information, either."

There was a moment of awkward silence.

"How about that salsa demonstration?" Manuel asked.

"Okay," Marisol said hastily, hoping the subject change would get everyone's attention off of Irena and Pablo's snipping at each other.

She helped clean up, wondering what had happened to have Irena and Pablo bickering with each other like this. She desperately hoped it had nothing to do with Celia.

She brought out a salsa CD and the portable CD player. Irena seemed agreeable to the demonstration. Marisol leaned over to Alex. "Would you mind demonstrating? We'll do the easiest steps we learned."

He looked at her, then turned his head to look at Pablo. A look passed between the cousins that Marisol couldn't read, and then Alex tuned back to her.

"Okay."

Marisol finished setting up the CD player, and then everyone took seats on the deck. Even the dogs, fed and walked, were quiet now and sat by her *Mamita*'s feet.

They took their positions, and Marisol nodded at Christa, who started the music.

The sultry musical notes flew out and surrounded them, and Alex took Marisol's hand, meeting her eyes.

They began the basic steps. Marisol felt wonderful, gliding along with Alex, her hand in his, the other on his shoulder. His steps were becoming more assured, although he still held himself stiffly. She knew he wasn't comfortable performing in front of everyone, and suspected he was doing this to take attention— at least some of the attention—away from Irena and Pablo.

They swayed, turned, and swayed. Marisol got a good look at Irena and Pablo. Pablo wasn't bad, but Irena had surprised her by catching on quickly in class, and now she was dancing the salsa very well for a beginner.

Alex deftly turned her, and she couldn't see the others. She caught his subtle but spicy aftershave. His hand was warm, the skin less smooth than hers but not rough.

She lifted her eyes and gazed into his.

Her breath caught. The look he gave her was one of yearning.

Then, suddenly, it was gone, masked by a casual expression. As if he wanted to hide his feelings.

Marisol hoped her feelings weren't transparent to everyone there. She smiled at Alex, trying to look like she was simply having a good time.

He slowly smiled down at her. And warmth rushed through her, down to her toes.

One look from the guy she loved, and it was impossible not to give him a great big smile.

The music was ending. They went into a final turn and dip, and stopped.

Applause burst out around them. Slowly Marisol and

Alex straightened. She felt her cheeks grow warm. Everyone was smiling and clapping.

And *Mamita* gave her a big wink.

"That was great," Marisol said, depositing the popcorn container they'd shared into a garbage holder as they left the cinema.

"Yes, very suspenseful," Alex agreed. He reached out and took hold of her small, feminine hand.

The movie had been exciting—a mystery thriller—and he'd enjoyed it when Marisol cuddled close during the scary parts.

It had caused him to forget his concerns about her, about their relationship. And about his cousin.

It had been apparent to him from the moment he saw Pablo this evening that his cousin was angry about something. He didn't show his anger readily, but Alex sensed it was there, simmering.

Had he had a fight with Irena?

And speaking of Irena, she hadn't looked too happy either. In fact, neither one seemed to be looking forward to their marriage very much, the last few times he'd seen them together.

And if they weren't . . . what the heck were they doing getting married? he wondered.

He'd have to make plans to see Pablo again in the next few days. After work. Or at least to talk to him on the phone, Alex thought as he strolled with Marisol toward his car. He had to persuade Pablo that if he was unhappy now, that wouldn't change. He should break his engagement—or at least postpone the wedding until his problems with Irena got worked out.

He glanced at Marisol. She was smiling softly, her face as beautiful as always, her expression, which was usually animated, now quietly content.

She must have sensed him studying her, because she turned her head and smiled.

Her smile was as bright as the moon, which was shining down on them from the soft summer night right now.

His inner organs melted. Marisol's smile did something to him. Made him feel wonderful, happy.

Made him wonder if love was possible, for him.

He sensed he was teetering on the edge of something. Something scary but enticing.

"Let's go for a walk," he suggested. "It's a nice evening." He pointed toward the shopping mall across the parking lot. "Just a short one."

"Sure," she said.

At a leisurely pace they moved toward the sidewalk in front of the stores. All the while, Alex's thoughts were spinning.

The thought that he shouldn't get more involved with Marisol kept repeating in his mind. Someone could end up getting hurt. Like him.

Like he'd been hurt before.

Not that he thought Marisol would deliberately hurt him. She was too sweet a person to do that. But she could also get hurt, if she cared for him and realized he didn't want to get too involved.

But there was also the thought—the desire—to get more involved.

"You look so pensive," she was saying. "What are you thinking about?"

They'd reached the sidewalk. The stores were closed now, only their names lit up against the dark, but between that and the moon there was plenty of light to see. It was as if she'd seen his thoughts on his face.

"Umm . . . I was thinking about Pablo," he said slowly. That was true—he had been thinking about his cousin.

"He and Irena didn't exactly look happy tonight, did they?" she asked. "And they were pretty quick to say they didn't want to come to the movies with us."

"No, they didn't look happy." He sighed. "My cousin and I are close, and I hate to see him troubled."

"Is he? Unhappy?" she continued.

"I'm afraid so. I think that they're—having problems," he said.

"They must be," Marisol said as they walked along, passing a few noisy teenagers coming out of a pizza place. "I don't know if he's the kind who would kiss Celia if he was happy with his engagement."

"No, I don't think he would," Alex agreed. "He would notice her—she's a nice-looking woman—but that would be it. I hope he hasn't developed a 'thing' for Celia. It reminds me of—" He stopped, both speaking and walking.

"It reminds you of . . . ," she prodded gently.

Maybe he should tell her. He wanted to tell her,

to explain why things between them should remain casually friendly. Why he didn't want a deep involvement.

"It reminds me of . . . Juanita," he admitted. There. He'd said it.

Marisol stared at him, her brow slightly furrowed. "Your ex-fiancée . . . who was so cold?"

"Yeah, well . . . ," he said. "I guess I should tell you the rest of that story."

"Tell me," she urged, her tone gentle.

They walked in silence for a few moments, and then he began. "What I told you was true—I realized Juanita was cold. And she wanted to marry me because she thought a nurse marrying a doctor was a good thing. We'd be financially successful, she'd live the kind of lifestyle she wanted."

Marisol made an indignant noise.

"There's more," he continued. "I finally decided this was not the woman I wanted to spend my life with. I was going to tell her, after work. I called and arranged to meet her the next evening. Then the next day, when I was working, I went to another area to speak to a surgeon about a patient. I was looking for him, and I opened a door—and there was Juanita, in the arms of another man. They were pretty hot and heavy."

"Oh, Alex," she whispered. They turned a corner and continued to walk past another set of stores.

"I couldn't believe it. Juanita, who was usually so cool, so restrained—I confronted them. She quite calmly told me she still wanted to marry me, but she thought she was entitled to a fling with Patrick, an orderly—for fun! Her exact words were that she thought before she settled down and got married that she should have one last hot affair." He heard the disgust in his own voice.

"That's terrible!" Marisol exclaimed, horrified by Juanita's actions and way of thinking. "How could she?"

"I thought so too. I told her I didn't want to marry someone who was cheating on me. We were through." He recognized the tension in his voice.

Marisol's hand tightened in his. "She didn't deserve you!" she exclaimed.

"I had already decided we were through, but this— this betrayal—really floored me. I was angry and disgusted—and couldn't believe I hadn't seen what was happening." Alex shook his head.

"She probably was very clever and hid it well from you," Marisol said. "She sounds calculating and cold enough to think she would get away with it."

"She would have, if I hadn't run into her," Alex said. He sighed, and letting go of her hand, shoved his hands in his pockets.

"But you were going to break it off with her, anyway," Marisol pointed out.

"Yes. My feelings had changed, but I still felt . . . like she took advantage of me."

"I can understand that." Marisol's words were soft. She paused, and turned to face him. He caught the scent of her exotic perfume, something feminine yet with a distinctly spicy note. Like Marisol.

"She was despicable," Marisol continued. "You're better off without her!"

"I know. But I still felt . . ." He paused, searching for the exact word.

"Betrayed?"

"Exactly." Marisol had nailed his sentiment. "Betrayed."

"And that's why . . . ," she started, then chewed her lip.

"That's why . . . ?" He waited for her to finish.

"That's why you don't trust women." Her voice was so low he leaned forward to catch her words.

She looked up at him. The moon lit her face, and she looked not just beautiful, but compassionate. She pulled his right hand from his pocket and took hold of it. Gazing up at him, she whispered, "You can trust me."

Something twisted inside him. He wanted to trust Marisol. He didn't think she would ever betray anybody. But . . . he had been wrong before.

"Trust me," she repeated. Her words were barely audible.

Alex stood still for a moment. She took a step closer.

He pulled her into his arms, and kissed her.

Kissing Marisol was like kissing no other woman. Her lips were soft and tender. He felt warmth in every part of him. Not just his physical body, but his soul.

She wrapped her arms around his neck, and pulled his head closer, kissing him back without reservation.

He reveled in the feel of her in his arms. If they could just stay like this, their arms around each other, he'd be happy.

A horn honked nearby.

He lifted his head and gazed into Marisol's eyes, realizing they were putting on a public display.

"I want to trust you," he said simply.

She smiled and, clinging to him, whispered back.

"That's a start."

If they kept standing here looking at each other he'd be kissing her again any second, and they could be standing here all night locked in each other's arms. With cars zooming by.

He stepped back slightly, still feeling dazed by the intensity of the kiss. Gripping her hand, he forced himself to say, "Let's keep walking. This isn't a very private place."

"You're right." She smiled and they strode back the way they came.

He tried to put his other thoughts into words. "This thing with Pablo and Celia—it's reminding me of Juanita."

"You mean Pablo is cheating on Irena?" Marisol sounded astonished.

"Or Celia is trying to seduce him."

She instantly came to the defense of her friend. "No, Celia would never do that! I know her."

"Well, okay, maybe she wouldn't." He wasn't so certain.

"But Pablo—are you saying that maybe he wants a last fling? Like Juanita did?" Now her voice held anger.

Was that what he was saying? Did he really believe his cousin would do that?

"I don't know," he said. "I'd like to believe Pablo would never do that. But he seems so tense lately, and I don't believe he's happy about his engagement. I just don't know."

Marisol gave him a sympathetic look. "I know how much you care about your cousin."

"We're only a year apart, and we're as close as I am to my brother—maybe even closer, since we did so many things together as kids."

"That doesn't mean he's not tempted to, well . . ." Her voice drifted off.

"To cheat on his fiancée?" Alex asked. "I'm still finding it hard to believe."

"One kiss doesn't mean he's cheating," Marisol said. "Look, why not let Pablo try to solve his own problem? Maybe he'll ask you for advice, maybe he won't." She smiled at him. "Now forget about Pablo and Irena and Celia. And most of all forget about Juanita."

He looked at her and smiled back. How could you not return a smile from Marisol Acevedo? Her smiles were positively bewitching.

That was it. He was bewitched, under her spell or something.

And enjoying every moment.

"I know how you can help me forget," he teased, and wrapping his arms around her, bent his head for another kiss.

Although Alex had to work most of the weekend, Marisol spoke to him several times. On Monday night he came over to watch a movie with her, and they cuddled close on the rec room couch.

She constantly felt like she was floating on air. She was in love, and she hoped—she thought—he was beginning to feel the same emotion. She guessed he was still fearful, and even if he recognized the feeling, he might not verbalize it for a while. But she was optimistic.

Tuesday's class was interesting. Marisol was keyed up, knowing she'd spend some time with Alex, and also on the alert for any sign of problems with Pablo or Irena or Celia. All her senses seemed to be working overtime, and she noticed every little thing.

Pablo and Irena came in separately. Although Pablo didn't seem as overtly unhappy as he had over the weekend, he was subdued.

Irena, on the other hand, was vivacious, more outgoing than normal. Marisol wondered if she was overreacting to a situation with Pablo. Irena spoke to Anne and Dominick, to Leo, even to Stella, as if she was having the time of her life.

Celia seemed like her usual outgoing self on the surface, but Marisol knew her friend well enough to recognize it was an act. Celia's eyes hinted at some kind of worry.

"How about if we get together for dinner on Wednesday?" she whispered to her during the first break. She knew Alex was working a twelve-hour shift the next day.

"Okay," Celia agreed.

As they took their places after the break, Marisol

found herself partnered with Leo. With a start she realized he hadn't called her for over two weeks and was no longer trying to monopolize her in class. This was a good thing, she thought. Perhaps he was finally getting the hint that she wanted to be merely a friend.

Feeling more at ease with him than she had since the class started, Marisol gave him a big smile. "How are you, Leo?"

He answered genially, telling her he thought he'd take a vacation soon. Then they concentrated on the salsa's steps.

Most of all, during class Marisol's senses picked up any little thing having to do with Alex. He spoke briefly with Pablo when he first came in, then came over to give her a quick hi and a smile. It was as if they shared a little secret.

During class she watched him dance with Stella, then Shannon. Sondra used him to demonstrate a move, and then he was partnered with Irena.

Near the end of class, Marisol got a chance to dance with him herself.

"You're really doing well!" she praised.

"Thanks." He gave her that smile that made her feel warm all over. "It's because I have a great teacher." He winked.

Marisol felt her whole body blush.

She also noticed throughout the class that Shannon and Xavier could hardly keep their eyes off each other, and knew that a romance was *definitely* brewing between them.

When the class ended, Alex lingered. As Irena and Pablo exited with Xavier and Shannon—Irena still talking animatedly—Alex moved toward Marisol.

"I'm only working a few hours on Saturday. Want to get together?" he asked.

"I'm working part of the day too, but I'd love to afterward," she replied.

Before she could say anything else, Stella came up to them with a question. By the time Marisol answered, Alex was waving and about to leave.

She hurried over to him. "Bye."

"I'll call you tomorrow," he promised.

She finished straightening up with Celia and Sondra, and then left. Driving home, Marisol felt exhilarated. Dancing with Alex, even talking to him—everything felt good, no, better than that—everything felt wonderful.

She said a silent prayer that Alex was feeling the same way.

Marisol and Celia had agreed to meet at a nearby mall after work and do a little shopping before eating at the food court.

She noticed at once that her friend seemed despondent. As they went through one store after another, she'd look at a shirt, or pick up a pair of jeans, and then put it back.

Marisol tried on a pair of sandals that were on sale, and seeing Celia's interest, urged her to try a pair too. They ended up getting the same pairs but in different colors—bright blue for Celia, hot pink for Marisol. That seemed to lift Celia's spirits a bit.

"Are you hungry?" Marisol asked as they strolled out of the store.

"Yes," Celia said.

They decided on Chinese food, and when they had their selections, brought their trays over to a table.

Marisol decided to start with a topic other than Celia's love life. "How's work going?" she asked, sipping her cola.

"All right. My boss said I'm getting a raise next week, since I'll be there three years then. Oh, and that insurance agent who's so snobby? She's moving out of state, and they're replacing her." Celia smiled briefly. "But . . . I'm still thinking of looking for another job. Something more interesting."

"Like what?" Marisol asked.

"Pablo was telling me about the mortgage business— did you know he's a very successful mortgage broker?"

Marisol shook her head. "Sorry, I have to admit I never asked."

"Well, he is. And it sounds fascinating. I could work as a secretary or get some training and be a loan processor. I think I'd really like it." Seeing something in Marisol's face, she added, "That doesn't mean I'll be working for Pablo. I think I need a change of pace, and the insurance office isn't very interesting."

"Well, maybe you should look into it," Marisol said cautiously.

"I'll probably look in another area."

Hearing the sudden, bitter note in her friend's voice, Marisol asked, "Why?"

Celia looked down, then back up. "I'm sure I'm in love with Pablo. And he's marrying Irena . . . I can't stick around and watch this." Her voice took on a despairing note.

"Oh, Celia," Marisol reached out and squeezed her friend's hand.

"I think I'll have to find a job outside of western Morris County. Maybe—down the shore. One of my cousins lives near Asbury Park. I could look down there."

"But your family and friends—" Marisol began.

Tears came into Celia's eyes, and she put down her fork. "It's—it's too painful to be here, where I would probably run into Pablo, or Irena. I've made so many bad choices in boyfriends the last few years . . . I think I need a fresh start."

Marisol leaned forward and squeezed her friend's hand. "I understand, Celia. But what if Pablo isn't happy with Irena?"

Celia stared at her. "Isn't—what do you mean?"

"I mean . . . it just seems to me he hasn't looked too happy around Irena lately." She didn't mention the dinner at her house to her friend, and didn't intend to unless Celia asked. "Irena doesn't seem really happy either."

"She seemed pretty bubbly to me last night," Celia stated.

"Last night . . . oh, I guess she did, but the week before they both seemed kind of tense. I get the feeling they're not super happy," Marisol finished.

Celia sighed. "If that's true, why doesn't one of them break it off?"

Marisol had no answer for that. "I don't know."

Celia smiled wanly. "I'd like to think there was some hope, but . . . I haven't seen any sign of it." She sighed.

"Don't give up hope," Marisol urged. She wondered if there was anything she could do to help her friend. "Maybe he'll realize there could be something special between you."

Celia switched topics abruptly. "Speaking of Pablo—how are you and his cousin? I saw the way he was looking at you yesterday."

Marisol didn't want to lie, but she didn't want to make a big deal about Alex while her friend was feeling so bad. She decided to try and play it down. "I really like him. But . . . he was hurt a long time ago by a girlfriend. I think he's still afraid to get too close."

"He may always be afraid," Celia said cynically.

Marisol stared, and Celia flushed.

"I'm sorry," Celia said. "I didn't mean that the way it came out."

Marisol felt a knot beginning in her stomach. Was Celia correct? "You could be right," she whispered.

"Marisol," Celia said, and Marisol could see her friend was feeling guilty about her remark. "If anyone could change Alex's mind, it's you."

"What do you mean?" Marisol asked.

"Because you're—you're so positive, and happy,

and—people like to be around you. I bet you will change Alex's outlook," Celia said rather fiercely.

Marisol desperately hoped so.

As she drove home from the mall, Marisol thought about Celia and Pablo. In some ways it was easier than thinking about Alex, and wondering if Celia was right. Would Alex always be fearful about love?

But Celia and Pablo . . . was there some way to get them together? She certainly didn't want to do anything that would jeopardize Pablo's engagement, but if it wasn't a solid one, was there some way to throw him together with Celia?

She couldn't think of any scenario that would be acceptable.

When she arrived home, Christa and her friend Laurie were hanging out in the living room, looking at fashion magazines.

"What'd you buy?" Christa asked.

Marisol displayed the sandals she'd purchased plus a cute bright pink top she'd gotten on sale.

Her mom came out of the kitchen. "Have a good shopping trip?" As soon as she'd seen Marisol's purchases, she said, "Come in the kitchen. I want to tell you about a phone conversation I had." She seemed a little perturbed.

Marisol followed her, with Pepé trailing after them. She took out a dog biscuit for him and then seated herself at the kitchen table when her mother offered her iced tea. "Thanks."

Her mom sat down beside her. "Leo's mother called a little while ago."

"Leo's mom?" Marisol's hand holding the glass stopped halfway to her lips.

"She was all agitated," her mother told her. "I told her you weren't home, but she said she had to speak to you."

"About what?" She slowly sipped the cool, refreshing iced tea.

"She says she's upset that you didn't return Leo's feelings."

"What!" Marisol stared at her mom, who suddenly smiled.

"I know, I know, it's strange, isn't it? For a mother to be calling someone and saying that?"

"Not just that." She took another sip, letting the icy beverage slide down her throat. In all the time she'd known Leo, she'd gotten the impression that his mother thought no one was quite good enough for her only child. Not Marisol, or anyone else for that matter. Mrs. Sanchez had definitely been cool toward her on the few occasions she'd been with the woman.

Marisol reminded her mother of that.

"I know, you told me that," her mother said. "So her comment surprised me too. Even though she'd be super lucky to ever get *you* as a daughter-in-law!" she added indignantly. "But then . . ." Her smile disappeared.

"Then—what?" Marisol pressed.

"I talked to her for a few minutes, and she admitted she was worried. About Leo. He's been going out late, and acting evasive, not answering questions, that sort of thing."

"Well, he's almost thirty. Old enough to not tell his parents every little thing he's doing," Marisol said dryly.

Marisol's grandmother entered the room. She must have heard some of the conversation from the deck, because she poured some iced tea from the pitcher and sat down at the table with her glass.

"Listen to this next part," *Mamita* put in. Obviously, Marisol's mother had already discussed it with her.

Her mom waved her hand. "Apparently Mrs. Sanchez is afraid Leo may be going out with a married woman."

"What?" Now Marisol was really shocked. "That doesn't sound like Leo."

"Well, that's what she's afraid of," her mother continued.

Marisol couldn't believe it. "It just doesn't sound like Leo. He's pretty conservative."

Mamita laughed. "Sometimes those are the ones most likely to act out."

Marisol's grandmother was a wise woman, but she still couldn't believe this of Leo. "Maybe, for some, but I don't think Leo would do that."

They spoke for a few minutes more, conjecturing why Mrs. Sanchez would think such a thing. Marisol finished her iced tea and wandered upstairs to put her purchases away. She had a busy day at the library tomorrow, with her first storytime for preschoolers for the summer. She showered, then lay on her bed with a mystery novel she'd started reading the other day.

But her thoughts kept returning to Leo. Both her grandmother and mother had noticed the same thing Marisol had days ago—that Leo was no longer persistently calling her.

Had his attention focused on another woman—a married woman?

Not that it was her problem, she concluded.

Now Celia—that was a problem that was much more important to her.

And Alex—she could only hope that he would learn to trust her, and their relationship really could develop.

She sighed. The book had a slow pace, and she just couldn't focus her attention on it. She got up and went to the computer, checking her e-mail and chatting on-line with Carina. Finally, she turned out the light and went to bed.

Her last waking thoughts were about Alex, and the hope that he would, as Celia remarked, change his outlook . . .

Thursday evening Alex came over to Marisol's home. Since they both had to be at work early on Friday, they stayed in and rented a movie on DVD.

For a change, her family tactfully left them in the basement rec room to watch the movie alone. Even Christa elected to stay in the living room or upstairs in her bedroom instead of barging in. Once, *Mamita* called down to say she'd made ice coffee if they wanted some, but otherwise they were left alone.

Marisol got to enjoy cuddling on the old couch with

Alex, watching a movie that was funny. Despite the fact that they weren't doing anything unusual, she enjoyed the evening as much as she had enjoyed going out for the gourmet dinner or going to the carnival. Just being with Alex was exciting.

Before he left, they shared some tender kisses, and agreed to go out for dinner on Saturday.

Marisol went to sleep that night feeling more hopeful than she had in days.

The following day was busy, but Alex still popped into her mind on a regular basis. Joyce teased her about going out with "the handsome doctor" on the weekend, and remarked that she'd never seen Marisol so excited about dating anyone.

"Even that Leo guy," she'd added.

Alex had called briefly late in the afternoon and told her he was working extra hours in the evening but was looking forward to seeing Marisol on Saturday. She felt like her whole being was glowing when she hung up the phone.

She spent a quiet evening at home, content to sit around and read and go on the computer. Christa was at the movies with some friends and her parents were visiting her brother and his family. Her grandmother was with Manuel at another neighbor's down the street, so she and Pepé had the house to themselves. Curled up on the living room couch, with Pepé snoozing beside her, Marisol allowed herself to daydream.

What if Alex really did fall in love with her . . . and came to trust her . . . and wanted to marry her? She pictured herself walking down the aisle, with a smiling Alex in a tuxedo waiting for her in front of the priest.

She must have started to doze off, because the sudden jingling of her cell phone startled her.

"Hola," she said, recognizing the number.

"Hola, Marisol. It's Celia."

Marisol leaned back on the couch's cushions. *"Hola,* Celia." Her friend sounded strange.

"I just wanted to tell you, I'm going down the shore this weekend and Monday too. I'm taking off from work. I'll be back Tuesday for our class."

"Oh, well, have a good time," Marisol said, wondering why Celia sounded odd.

"I'm going to look at places to live, and look for a job on Monday. I have two interviews lined up already."

That made Marisol sit up. "Celia, I—I don't know what to say. I mean, I want you to be happy, but—if you move, I won't get to see you much," she added, somewhat lamely.

She pictured Celia shrugging. "I can't help it. I have to do something, Marisol. I'm going crazy. Last night I was at Wal-Mart and I ran into Pablo and Irena." There was a heavy sigh as she finished.

"And . . . ?" Marisol probed.

"I can't take it. I—it hurts too much to see them together. To see *her* bossing him around. And they're still engaged. No, I don't want to be in this situation." She sounded now like she was sniffling.

"Oh, Celia." Marisol sighed herself. "If you were here, I'd give you a big hug. It must be painful."

"It is. And I don't want this to keep happening. Irena said they're going to be living here in town, which means I'll be running into them. I can't do it."

"What about your family?" Marisol asked.

"I'll tell them I'm moving when I have a job. They don't know yet."

"I'll miss you, but I do understand," Marisol said.

At the same time, a little voice inside asked her, could the same thing happen to *her*?

She quickly smothered the voice with a mental pillow.

"I know you do," Celia said. "And I just hope your relationship works out, Marisol, and you don't have to go through anything like this."

It hurt to even consider that possibility.

Marisol swallowed. "I hope I won't," she said, making an effort to keep her voice steady. "But—are you sure of this, Celia? Maybe you should wait."

"I've made up my mind. Anyway, Marisol, it's not like I'm going to California. I'll be a few hours away, but you can come down and visit me."

"Of course I will," Marisol said. Maybe once her friend looked around, she'd realize she didn't really want to move.

Or maybe this was the best thing for her.

They spoke for only a few more minutes. Marisol wished her luck, and then hung up.

She stared at the shiny metallic cell phone in her hands, smoothing her fingers over the back.

Perhaps Celia had the right idea. Start fresh, where

she didn't have to see the man she loved marrying someone else.

Would she be in that situation herself someday?

Marisol shivered. Pepé looked up suddenly from his
corner of the couch, as if reading her thoughts.

"Shh, baby," she said, and stroked the little dog. He
sighed, closed his eyes, and drifted back to sleep.

But her own thoughts continued to stumble. Alex—
she couldn't picture him marrying someone else. There
was no one else in his life, and she knew he was fond of
her, maybe felt something more.

But that didn't mean he'd want to get married, like
she did.

Would she someday end up like Celia, moving to avoid
encounters with a man she loved but couldn't have?

She had no answer to that question.

Chapter Eight

Alex was a few minutes late pulling up to Marisol's home. He'd tried about five times to get hold of Pablo during the day, hoping they could make plans to get together again, and talk about Pablo's engagement. He left messages two of those times. He knew Pablo often worked part of the day on Saturdays, but had hoped they'd at least speak before he headed out.

However, he hadn't heard back from his cousin, so realizing he was running late, he'd given up and headed to Marisol's.

Now he hopped out of his car, eager to see her. Despite his hectic week at work and the troubling feelings about his cousin, Marisol had been constantly on his mind. He was determined to enjoy the evening with her and not worry about his cousin's problems, or anything else.

She opened the door as soon as he rang the doorbell, and he stepped into the cool interior as Pepé bounded around him.

Wearing a black and white print dress with a red beaded necklace and matching bracelet, she looked fashionable and feminine. Her dark hair curled at her shoulders, and her gorgeous face wore the sunny smile he always looked forward to seeing. The scent of her feminine perfume engulfed them both. She was gorgeous and alluring.

"Hi," she murmured.

He didn't think, just acted. He pulled her into his arms and planted a light kiss on her luscious red lips.

Pepé jumped at him.

She stepped back. "Pepé," she scolded lightly.

Alex was suddenly conscious that others were nearby. He reached down and patted the little dog, who seemed content with getting some notice, and then bounded away.

"Dr. Lares!" Marisol's grandmother called to him from the living room sofa.

He greeted her, and Marisol's mother, who was coming out of the kitchen.

Turning to Marisol, he asked, "Shall we go?"

Everyone told them to have a good time as they left.

Once in the car, he asked Marisol about going to the Mexican restaurant. Since it was early for a Saturday night, they would be able to get a table right away.

He'd had a reason for picking this restaurant, though he wasn't going to tell her till later. This was the place where they'd eaten after class several weeks ago with the others, and the restaurant featured dancing. He thought Marisol would really enjoy that, and after almost six weeks of classes, he finally felt confident enough to get on the dance floor with Marisol in public.

The drive took only a few minutes. Marisol asked about his week, and he described the long hours he'd put in. "They changed my schedule yesterday. I crawled home at nine last night and was in bed by ten o'clock," he admitted. "One of the patients who came in was a neighbor of my parents—he'd had a heart attack. We'd told him months ago when he was over he should stop smoking, but . . ." Alex shook his head.

"He didn't listen?" Marisol asked.

"No. But yesterday, when he was over the worst of it, he grabbed my hand and said, 'Doc, if I survive, I'll quit smoking.' I hope he does."

"I hope so too," Marisol said, and laid her fingers on his hand.

Her light touch did something to him. Warmed him all over, just like her smile did. It made him think of sunshine and bright music.

They were led to their table, and sat down. He asked Marisol about the summer reading program.

"I started my preschoolers' storytime," she told him. "It was crowded but it went well. The summer reading program for the elementary school kids officially starts next week. We have a lot of kids signed up!" She looked happy about that.

They started to talk about the books they were reading

now, and went on to compare books they'd read recently. Marisol read a wide variety of books, which wasn't surprising, being a librarian.

It was nice to have someone to discuss books with, he thought as they were brought their appetizers of quesadillas. He'd found very few people who liked to read as much as he did.

And they both enjoyed mysteries. Marisol recommended a new author he should try. "And what are you reading right now?" she asked.

"Besides a medical journal, I'm reading a book about the history of aviation. I like reading about scientific discoveries," he added.

"That sounds fascinating," Marisol said.

He relaxed, and enjoyed the food and conversation. That was one of the best things about Marisol, he thought. You could be yourself with her, and relax and have a good time. He didn't feel like he had to work at impressing her, or like she was looking at him with dollar bills in her eyes. She wanted to know him, the real Alejandro Lares.

A DJ sat in the corner of the restaurant, and near the end of their meal he started playing music.

Marisol was sipping her piña colada, and he lifted his and touched it to her glass.

"To you," he said.

Her eyebrows rose delicately. "To me?"

"Yes." He grinned, then took a sip of his drink. The pineapple and coconut mixture tasted refreshing and sweet. "To you, Marisol, the best salsa teacher around . . . and the most beautiful."

She smiled, her cheeks growing rosy in the dim light. "*Gracias.*"

"Would you like to dance?" he asked.

"I'd love to," she answered swiftly.

The music that was playing now was a simple, slow tune, the kind Alex really preferred. A romantic one. A person could dance gently to music like this, stepping easily over the dance floor without any special routines, holding his partner close.

He led the way to the dance floor behind an older couple. Marisol stepped easily into his arms, and he pulled her close.

She fit neatly into his arms. Although she was shorter than him, she was wearing heels, and his lips grazed her satiny hair. He caught the faint scent of a shampoo that smelled like pineapples.

He brushed her hair with a soft kiss.

He felt a tremor go through Marisol, and her fingers tightened in his. He thought he heard the softest of sighs from her.

She felt light and feminine and perfect in his arms. He could stay on the dance floor with her all night if they danced just like this.

But the music ended a few minutes later. He raised his head and met Marisol's eyes. She wore a dreamy expression.

The DJ started a salsa number. Feeling more daring than usual, Alex suggested they dance to this too, and Marisol instantly agreed.

The song was one they'd done in class last week. The

fast pace had him scrambling, trying to do the correct steps and not collide with any of the other couples on the dance floor. Or with Marisol. Although she seemed remarkably able to avoid being trampled.

He recognized that she was leading a little, trying to guide him surreptitiously in the steps of the dance. The music was faster than most of the songs they'd danced to in class, and he was grateful that she was helping him.

She smiled at him. "You're doing fine," she whispered.

He didn't think so, though, and felt relief when the number finally ended.

"Let's take a break," he said.

She didn't object as he led her by the hand back to the table. Once there, she beamed at him.

"I like dancing with you," she said simply.

"I do too," he admitted. "I never thought I'd like dancing this much—"

A persistent vibrating in his jacket pocket alerted him that he had a call on his cell phone. He'd turned it to silent mode, not wanting any interruptions. But he had left it on in case there was news about his parents' neighbor.

"I'm sorry," he apologized. "I'm getting a call. I'm not on call tonight, but I just want to see if this is about Edwin—my parents' neighbor, the one who was my patient yesterday."

"No problem," Marisol said.

In the dim light, it was hard to see. He pressed a button and looked at the number that had called. It was Pablo's.

"It's my cousin," he said, placing the cellphone back

in his pocket. "He's probably returning my call. I want to try to get together with him in the next few days."

"Do you want to take it?" she asked.

He shook his head. "I'll call him back later." Much later, he thought. Like tomorrow.

Tonight, he wanted to concentrate on the very special woman who was with him.

They ate their dinner, enjoying the spicy food, and talking about the salsa class and some of the people in it. He was surprised when Marisol told him that Shannon and Xavier were dating. He had noticed them acting friendly at the carnival and in class, but hadn't thought much about it.

They avoided the topics of Pablo and Irena and Celia.

They got up to dance to another slow tune. Afterward they enjoyed watching a couple doing a dance that Marisol informed him was a tango.

They lingered over coffee and ice cream. Halfway through, Marisol declared she couldn't eat another bite.

"Everything was delicious," she said. "But I'm stuffed!"

"I'm almost there too," he admitted.

He had planned to ask Marisol if she'd like to go to the park in town. They could walk around on the paths and get some time alone together, without interruptions from her various family members. Not that he disliked her family—it was just that he would like time alone with Marisol, to put his arm around her and stroll among the flowers . . .

He opened his mouth to suggest the idea as Marisol put down her coffee cup with a clink of china.

"I have a plan for where we can go after dinner," she said, smiling. Her eyes gleamed in the dim light.

Intrigued, he asked, "Where?"

"It's a surprise."

He wasn't too crazy about surprises. He couldn't imagine where she would suggest going. But with Marisol, he trusted it wouldn't be anything bad.

He paid the check for dinner. Leaving the restaurant, they walked hand in hand. The evening had grown dark with bluish-gray clouds and an accompanying strong wind.

"We're going to get rain," Marisol said, glancing at the sky.

"Where are we going?" he asked.

She flashed him a smile. "Not far."

As they got into the car, his phone vibrated again. A quick look revealed it was once again Pablo.

Marisol had raised her eyebrows. "Your patient?"

"No, my cousin . . . I'll call him tomorrow." Maybe, Alex thought, Pablo wanted to talk to him as much as he wanted to speak with his cousin.

He started the car and pulled out of the parking lot. Marisol directed him to go back to the heart of Dover. Once back on Blackwell Street, she had him go straight until she told him to enter a parking lot.

"We're by the dance studio," he said.

She smiled, and held up her ring of keys. They jangled

in her hand. "That's right. I'm giving you a private lesson."

Marisol watched Alex's expression as she said the words. Would the usually staid Alejandro Lares object to this impulsive-sounding idea?

Not that it had been an impulse. She had thought this out carefully. A romantic interlude, dancing with Alex. Just the two of them, plenty of space to pivot and whirl, no interference from meddling family members . . .

"I have Sondra's permission to use the studio," she added. "It's just you and me."

A smile lit up Alex's face. "Let's go."

They walked the half block to the dance studio, and she opened the door. The lobby was dark, with the blinds closed and what was left of daylight barely filtering through.

As she closed the door, a sudden flash almost made her jump. Lightning.

The boom that followed sounded close by.

Marisol fumbled with the switch, and then the lobby lights came on.

"C'mon," she said, leading the way into the studio.

She turned on only about half of the lights, deliberately leaving the studio partially in darkness for a more romantic atmosphere. Moving to the CD player, she quickly switched it on and found the CD she wanted.

She turned back to Alex and walked the few steps to where he was lounging against the wall, studying her. A smile played at his mouth, as if he was slightly amused.

She touched his face gently with her hand.

"Come, salsa with me," she whispered.

He caught her hand, planting a kiss on her palm. At his touch, a shiver went up her spine.

"With pleasure," he whispered in Spanish. In his native tongue, the words were even more enticing and romantic.

This time he led her into the center of the room. Surrounded by shadows, they took their positions, and when the hot music started, Alex moved with her.

The teacher part of her noticed that he was more sure of himself, his steps firmer and more confident, here in the empty studio with no one else watching. They danced as if they had been dancing together for years, each motion in sync.

The emotional part of her felt thrills as they turned, pulled apart slightly, then came together closer than before. She smelled his spicy, masculine aftershave. His leg brushed against hers. His hand tightened, and their eyes met and held.

They turned, then he drew her closer. Marisol caught her breath. She swore she could feel the rhythm of Alex's heartbeat.

And hers was keeping exactly the same pace, right in time to the music.

His face was shadowy, his eyes dark. He was every Latin movie star she'd ever had a crush on rolled into one. And so much more.

They parted, stepped in unison, and then he pulled her closer again.

She could almost swoon from the pleasure.

The music slowed, and faded. All she could think was, *I want to do this again. And again.*

She felt a tremor in Alex's chest. No, not a tremor. Something was vibrating in his pocket.

Alex muttered something.

His cell phone . . . of course.

Marisol sighed as Alex stepped back. He definitely looked annoyed.

"Sorry. It's my phone," he said, his voice a low rumble.

She nodded, unable to speak. All she wanted to do was go back into his arms and repeat the dance. Forget further lessons, she was content to keep doing this one dance they were doing so well together over and over again.

Alex fumbled with his phone, and when he pulled it out, he stared at it with almost a distasteful expression.

"It's—" He paused. "No, it's not the hospital. It's Pablo again." Now he frowned. "That's the third time—" He looked up, meeting her eyes, and she recognized the flash of concern in them.

"Maybe something's wrong," he said. "My family . . ."

"Go ahead, call him," she urged. She didn't want him distracted by worries. And maybe there was something wrong.

"I'm sorry," he repeated, then dialed back the number that had called.

Marisol watched as Alex, looking both annoyed and anxious, put the phone to his ear. Pablo must have picked up immediately, because Alex nearly snapped, "Pablo. You got me at a bad time. *Que pasa?*"

She watched as he listened, and then his body went suddenly rigid.

"What?"

Her heart began to beat harder. Was something wrong? Someone in his family ill?

Alex had raised his eyes to meet hers.

"Irena? And—"

She saw shock register on his face. "You're kidding." Her heartbeat sped up.

Alex stared at her, his hand clutching the cellphone.

"What is it?" she asked anxiously.

"It's Irena. She's eloped."

"Eloped?" Marisol repeated, wondering if she'd heard wrong. "You mean with Pablo?"

"No." He took a shuddering breath.

"Who—" She began.

"With Leo."

Chapter Nine

"*W*hat?*" Marisol's voice came out as a screech. How could—there must be some mistake—

Alex spoke rapidly into the phone. "I'm with Marisol. I'll call you back later." His words were clipped. He continued to stare at Marisol as he flipped the phone shut.

"Irena and Leo?" she gasped. How could that be? That Irena would elope, with Leo of all people.

But even as her thoughts tumbled and collided, a part of her knew it was possible.

Irena hadn't been happy with Pablo. And although she hadn't flirted with Leo, she had been talking to him during the last class, and at dinner . . .

And Leo, conservative Leo?

Not so conservative, after all. As *Mamita* had said, those were the ones you had to watch—the ones likely to "act out."

172

And Marisol remembered that Leo's parents were concerned about the sneaking around he'd been doing, suspecting he was with a married woman—

Not a married woman. An engaged one. Irena.

She swallowed, her eyes still fastened on Alex, who looked as shocked as she was herself.

"Irena. And Leo?" She shook her head. "I mean, I knew Irena and Pablo weren't too happy, but I never suspected that she would run off."

"With Leo." He made Leo sound like a dread disease.

"How did Pablo find out?" she asked, her voice raspy.

"He hadn't heard from her all day and she didn't return his call this afternoon. When he went to check his mail late in the afternoon, there was a note in his mailbox. She said"—he paused, then continued—"she realized she wasn't really in love with Pablo, and that she was in love with Leo. She wanted a grand romance, and she and Leo had run off to get married."

"Where?" Marisol asked, but she suspected she knew. "Las—"

"Las Vegas," he answered at the same time.

Las Vegas, the place Irena had said she thought sounded so exciting and romantic.

"She left a note for her family too; she didn't even tell them," Alex continued. "Pablo went right over there to talk to her and they had just found a letter she left in her room."

"Poor Pablo," she whispered. But a little part of her brain was saying, *No, not poor Pablo. He doesn't love*

Irena. And then another part said, *Celia! You should tell Celia!*

For the moment, she ignored those thoughts. "How is Pablo?"

"In shock, I imagine." Alex sounded a little in shock himself. As Marisol studied him, she noticed his mouth had become set in a grim line. "How could she do this to him?"

"You're right, she should have told him in person," Marisol agreed. "But—they *were* having trouble."

"This is no way to handle the situation." Alex was shaking his head. He stopped and stared at the cell phone, still in his hand. "I think he needs me."

"Of course," Marisol agreed, but her heart was sinking. Not just because Alex wanted to go give his cousin support, and their romantic evening was cut short. No, it was Alex's expression, which was growing darker by the minute, as ominous as the clouds outside which were rumbling again.

And she could guess why.

Pablo had been betrayed by Irena.

Just as Alex had been, once.

Her blood was slowly freezing.

Oh no, oh no. Was Alex going to go back to thinking that women were all like Juanita?

She refused to believe that he would think that way. After all, it was Pablo who was involved, not him. And Pablo hadn't exactly been happy in his relationship lately.

Still, to have your fiancée run out on you . . .

"Would you like me to come with you?" she asked Alex.

"No." He shook his head. "I better take you home, then get right over to see him. He's at his parents' house right now. He just came back from Irena's house, and her mother's hysterical."

Leo's mother would be too, Marisol suspected.

She nodded. "All right." She strove to keep the disappointment from her voice. "You're a good friend to Pablo," she added.

Alex nodded.

She turned off the music and lights, and they left the now-dark studio. Outside, the wind whipped at her dress, the clouds reflecting Alex's bleak mood.

They drove in silence the few minutes to Marisol's house. Rain was just beginning to sprinkle when Alex pulled into the driveway.

He walked her up to the door. "I'm sorry our evening was cut short."

Marisol hoped that was true regret she heard in his voice. "I am too," she replied softly. Turning, she gently touched his cheek. "Tell Pablo I'm thinking of him. Take care," she finished.

He bent his head and gave her a swift kiss. Then he turned and hurried back to his car.

Marisol stared after him.

She felt like the wind was blowing in something bad. Like things had taken a turn for the worse, and not just for Pablo. For all of them.

And yet, Pablo hadn't been happy with Irena.

Raindrops hit her face, and with a sigh, she let herself into the house.

Pepé ran up to greet her. The house was silent except for his happy barks, and she picked him up and pet him. "Let's go outside quickly, Pepé, before it rains hard," she said, and took him to the back door for a quick walk.

Within minutes they were back inside, and Marisol gave the little dog a treat before slowly trudging up the stairs to her room.

The evening had started out so hopefully. She had been so excited about her date with Alex, her plan to dance with him. And in the darkened studio, their dance had been intensely romantic. She could still feel his arms around her . . .

Sighing again, she shed her clothes and got into old jeans and a pale blue T-shirt.

Celia. She should call Celia and tell her what had happened.

She reached for her cell phone and scrolled down to Celia's number. Celia answered on the second ring.

Quickly, Marisol told her what had occurred.

Celia gasped, and kept repeating, "I can't believe it!"

Hope had begun to stir in Marisol—hope for her friend. "Maybe, Celia, this is the time for you to tell Pablo how you feel—maybe things can work out for the two of you!"

"Oh, Marisol!" Celia said, her voice sounding close to

a wail. "I love Pablo, but I don't want to be the rebound woman. I want him to love me because I'm me, not as a substitute for Irena."

"I don't think he cares for Irena," Marisol said. "I haven't seen him yet, but I'm guessing he's just in shock. I have a feeling he's not as hurt as Alex thinks."

"I don't know." Celia sounded doubtful. "In the meantime, I have two interviews on Monday, and I think I found a nice apartment."

They spoke for a few more minutes, and then Celia got off, saying she wanted time to think.

Marisol settled down to read, the rain hitting the window providing background noise. But she couldn't concentrate on her book.

It didn't take long for word to get around about Irena and Leo. By the next afternoon, it seemed the entire community knew.

Marisol had of course told her family when they came home from their various activities. But as they approached church Sunday morning one of her mother's friends had run up with the news. Apparently Irena's mother was beside herself and several of her friends had rushed to provide comfort last night. Now they were all repeating the scandalous tale.

After the Mass, Marisol and her family returned home, and the phone began to ring and ring. Carina dropped in and joined them in the kitchen as they ate sandwiches for lunch.

"This is hot news," *Mamita* said. She sounded amused by it all. "I must say I am surprised, even though you never know what will happen . . ."

"I'm surprised too," Marisol admitted.

Marisol's mother grimaced. "It's a good thing he didn't try to persuade you to elope, Marisol. I would be having a fit just like Irena's mother."

"I have a feeling it was more Irena's idea," Marisol said.

"Marisol wouldn't elope," Carina said, reaching for the bowl of corn chips.

"I remember a friend of mine eloped when we were young.," *Mamita* said. "In those days, it was more common, especially if the family of the girl didn't like the man she was seeing. Nobody lived together—they would take off and elope."

"I can imagine what Leo's mother is saying," Marisol said, rolling her eyes.

"Hmph," her mother said. "I hear Irena's mother is very upset because they had this beautiful wedding planned. And because they should have gotten married in the church."

"Well, I predict Marisol will have a beautiful wedding," *Mamita* said, smiling at her.

"I have no plans to get married," Marisol said hastily. At least, not now she didn't. But she hoped . . .

As soon as lunch was over she and Carina escaped upstairs. They discussed the situation for a while, then Carina left to visit her grandparents.

Shortly afterward, Marisol got a call on her cell phone,

and was surprised when she picked up and found Pablo on the other end.

"How are you?" she asked sympathetically.

"Fine." He sounded tense, though, despite his word. "I've been trying to reach Celia. Do you know where she is? I tried her cell phone but I only get voice mail. Then I tried her phone number at home but no one answered, so I left a message."

Marisol felt torn. She wanted Pablo to get in touch with her friend. But she had to respect Celia's wishes on the subject.

"She's away for a couple of days," she said cautiously, seating herself on her bed. "If she calls me I'll tell her you're trying to reach her."

"Thanks," Pablo said, then fell silent.

"How are you doing, really?" Marisol asked gently when he said nothing more.

He hesitated. "All right, I guess. I was—kind of shocked. Irena eloping? It—it's just hard to believe." He gave a wry laugh. "I should have known. She was getting evasive all of a sudden, and spending less time with me—when she used to want to spend *all* of her time with me. I should have seen it coming," he finished.

"No one saw it coming," Marisol said, trying to make him feel better. "No one suspected. And Leo—that was, well, quite a shock!"

"Absolutely. I can't help wondering—why Leo? I mean, what does he have that I don't?"

Marisol's heart went out to him. This couldn't be an easy thing to deal with, even if Pablo had begun to feel differently about the girl he was supposed to marry. It had to hurt on top of the shock.

"I don't know," she replied honestly. "I think you have more personality than Leo. Maybe she liked the fact that he's an accountant?"

"Who knows?" His voice sounded dark. Again, there was a moment of silence.

"How are your parents taking this? And Irena's parents?" Marisol asked, sensing he needed someone to speak to and was reluctant to get off the phone.

"My parents are mad—but, I think, also a little relieved. My father said he never cared for Irena much, and this goes to prove he was right about her character. My mother is just plain mad that she would do this."

"I can understand that," Marisol said, leaning back against her pillows.

"And Irena's parents—they're so upset. I think her father's mad at me, as if it's my fault." He made a snorting sound. "And her mother just cries about how Irena was supposed to have this beautiful wedding, and her only daughter eloped to some chapel in Las Vegas that probably isn't even a church."

"I'm sure they got married legally," Marisol said. "I can't imagine either of them not doing that."

"Yeah, but not the church wedding her mother had planned for her only daughter." Pablo sighed. "I was over there last night, and again this morning. Irena called briefly around noon to say they were married last night. So it's a done deal. All her mother could do was cry."

"I'm sorry," Marisol repeated.

"You have nothing to apologize for."

"I know." She sighed. "It's just—I feel bad for you, and everyone. And—they met in my class."

"Feel bad for Leo," Pablo cut in. "He's the one stuck with her now."

Marisol suspected Pablo was hurting and his snappy comeback was just to cover up his own confused feelings. She still hoped he cared for Celia, but she suspected Celia was right. His dating her on the rebound wasn't a very good basis for a relationship. Maybe if some time passed . . .

"Marisol?"

"Yes?" she responded.

"I'm sorry, I didn't mean to snap at you," he said.

"No problem," she said, keeping her voice sympathetic.

"I really want to talk to Alex, but he was on call this morning and got called in to work. Something about a bus accident and a lot of injuries."

"Oh," she said. "Maybe I'll call him tonight to see how he's doing." It would give her a good excuse, she mused.

"I guess we both will. Hey, thanks for listening to me complain."

"That's okay," she said gently. "If you need to talk to me later, just call."

When Pablo hung up, she shut her phone and stared at it for a long time.

She did feel a little responsible, since Leo had taken

the class to be near her. Although she knew, intellectually, this whole thing was not her fault, she couldn't help feeling a little guilty.

Would Pablo and Celia find their way to each other through this mess?

And what about her and Alex? Would she and Alex find their way through this mess?

Chapter Ten

Marisol was as nervous about Tuesday's salsa class as she had been on her first day as an assistant teacher.

The minute she walked in, Sondra nearly pounced. "Is it true?" the teacher asked anxiously.

She didn't have to ask what. Sondra and her husband lived in town, and knew a lot of people.

"Yes," Marisol answered.

"Oh, *Dios,*" Sondra whispered, looking distressed. "And to think this happened in my class . . ."

Celia entered, and as they poured lemonade, she changed the topic to the weather.

It was no surprise that Irena and Leo were the hot topic of discussion as the students filtered in. The whispers started as soon as everyone entered, and they grew louder as more people filed in.

"I was totally shocked," Marisol heard Anne say to Stella. "I thought Irena was devoted to Pablo."

"I saw her looking at Leo last week, and he returned her look . . . it was obvious something was going on," Shannon said.

Pablo did not show up for class.

Of course, she shouldn't be surprised, Marisol thought as they took their places. He had been taking the salsa lessons for his wedding . . . a wedding that would never happen now.

Alex did show up. He came in just as the class started. He looked tired and tense. She gave him a smile, hoping his expression would lighten. He smiled briefly at her, then turned his attention to Sondra, who was reviewing some steps.

She noticed as class went on that Celia was acting as lighthearted as usual—even more so, she observed. As if she didn't want anyone to think she had a care in the world.

But Marisol suspected most of Celia's thoughts were centered on Pablo.

She wondered as they reviewed last week's steps if Alex had come just to see her. She hoped so. After all, he'd taken the class because Irena and Pablo had pressured him into it for their wedding.

She forced herself to concentrate on the dance steps. She managed well, but felt relief when the first break came.

Of course, most of the discussion during the break still centered around the eloping couple.

Marisol went to get some cold water, and had a moment alone with Celia.

"How are you?" she asked, her voice pitched low.

Celia sighed. "Confused."

"Did Pablo reach you on your cell phone?"

"Yes, but . . . he wants to come over and speak to me, and I don't know what to do." Celia bit her lip. "I want to see him, but . . . you know what I'm afraid of."

Marisol nodded as Shannon approached. "I know, you don't want to be his second choice."

"Yes," she whispered. Then Celia turned her smile on Shannon. "That's something, isn't it, about Leo and Irena? Who would have thought . . . ?"

Marisol admired Celia for being so forthright about a topic that was obviously bothering her. Xavier joined them, and told them that his mother was a distant cousin to Irena's father.

"Irena's parents are acting as if the world has come to an end," he said.

Shannon rolled her eyes. "Maybe they think it has."

"Her mother's overly dramatic," he said, obviously thinking the elopement wasn't as big a deal as some of Irena's family did.

Marisol stepped back, seeing Alex approaching. When he reached her, she said softly, "Hi."

"Hi," he responded, and reaching for a cup, poured himself water.

"I heard you worked a lot of hours on Sunday," she said, "with that bus accident."

"Yes, Pablo told me he spoke to you." Alex sounded weary, and looked as tired as he sounded.

"I heard no one died," Marisol went on, sensing he didn't want to talk too much about Pablo, "but that there were a lot of injuries."

"Yes, mostly broken bones, and a couple of concussions and abrasions. Fortunately no injuries were life-threatening."

"That's good," she said.

Behind Marisol an older woman talking with some of the other students exclaimed, "Irena, that young woman who's engaged—you mean her?" Obviously, it was still a big topic. And there were a few people who hadn't heard . . . yet.

"Yes," Stella responded, "she ran off—"

Alex grimaced.

Well, there was no avoiding the topic, it seemed. "How is Pablo?" Marisol asked, keeping her voice down.

"I guess okay . . . we've only talked briefly. I worked all day Sunday, Monday, and part of today. He's been throwing himself into work the last couple of days," Alex said. "I hope I'll get to see him one night this week."

Sondra was clapping her hands to get the class going again.

The variations were getting harder for the class, and Marisol went from one student to another, helping them as Sondra reviewed the earlier lesson. By the second break more of the students had caught on, but after the break Marisol continued to help people. By the end of class, as Sondra praised everyone, Marisol felt relief—and weariness. Not only had the evening's lesson been difficult, but the atmosphere had been heavy with the heat of gossip and innuendo regarding the eloping couple.

Marisol couldn't wait to go home, but people lingered, talking and speculating about Leo and Irena. Alex moved toward her.

"I'm beat," he said. "I'm going home to sleep for twelve hours—I hope."

She could see how fatigued he looked. "I'm glad you made it to class," she said softly.

He gave her a brief smile. "I'll call you tomorrow."

"Okay, bye," she said, and watched as he left the room.

She didn't have a good feeling. Alex looked more than tired. His expression was strained, and troubled, she thought.

Well, exhaustion could do that to you, she knew. Or stress.

She went back to straightening up, saying good-bye to Shannon and Xavier and others who were slowly leaving the room. It was warm and stuffy despite the air-conditioning. She suspected it wasn't just because people had been dancing up a storm. The atmosphere had been hot.

Finally, no one was left but Marisol, Celia, and Sondra. When they were finished, Sondra turned off the air conditioner and the lights, and locked up. They proceeded to the parking lot and said good-byes. Marisol guessed that Celia was just as glad to go home and have some quiet time as she was.

She couldn't quite shake this feeling that there was more to Alex's demeanor than simple weariness.

She switched on the radio to a local rock station. Once home, she was glad to see her parents and grandmother absorbed in a TV show. She greeted them and ran upstairs, saying she was hot and needed to shower.

Later, she sat at her computer, surfing the Web listlessly. Christa was on her cell phone chatting with a friend on the other side of the long room, and Marisol felt she could finally unwind and have some time alone.

But all she could think of was Alex.

The following day Marisol spoke briefly with Alex. Although he was supposed to work only part of the day, several emergencies and the fact that they were still shorthanded in the ER meant he had to put in more time at work. It was Wednesday, the Fourth of July, usually a busy day at the hospital. Marisol ended up going to the fireworks at the nearby county college with Carina and a few other friends. They invited Celia to join them but she declined. Marisol didn't want to stay home and mope, and was determined to have a good time. But Alex was never far from her thoughts.

Alex picked her up in the early evening on Thursday and they went to see a movie that turned out to be lackluster and predictable.

"Why don't we get an ice cream," he suggested as they left the cinema.

Marisol agreed, and they drove the short distance to an outdoor ice cream place that had been there for decades.

Marisol noticed that Alex was quieter than usual, and seemed tense.

Once they were sitting on one of the wooden benches outside, Alex said quietly, "I wanted to talk to you."

A knot formed in her stomach. It wasn't just the words—it was Alex's tone. He sounded serious. Too serious.

"Yes?" she asked softly, her voice pitched low.

"About—us." He looked away, then back at her again.

She waited, the knot in her stomach tightening.

"I . . . I care about you, Marisol. A lot." He reached out and took hold of her left hand, the one not holding her ice cream cone.

Relief flooded her. Maybe he was trying to tell her something she wanted to hear?

"But . . . ," he continued.

Her stomach plummeted.

"But . . . ?" she asked when he fell silent. It wasn't like Alex to speak so hesitantly.

"I'm just . . . unsure about our relationship. About the future." He met her look with his own.

"What do you mean?" she asked.

Could this be what she had always feared? His inability to trust women? It was the fear she had pushed to the back of her brain when she first learned about Irena running off with Leo.

"I mean . . ." He looked uncomfortable under her scrutiny. "I care for you, Marisol, and I never want to hurt your feelings. Not in a million years. But this relationship—" He waved his ice cream cone slightly, and some mint chocolate chip slid down the cone. "I'm not sure we should continue . . . at least not at this pace. I think we need to slow things down, put the brakes on our relationship."

It was as if a hole had suddenly opened on the ground beneath her feet. Marisol felt like she was plummeting downward. This is how Alice in Wonderland must have felt, she thought numbly.

Marisol could only stare at Alex.

"Why?" she asked, almost choking on the one word.

"Why? Because . . . I'm just not sure. I had doubts about getting involved with another woman since Juanita, and now—if we stay involved, someone's going to get hurt. You could get hurt. I don't know if I can give to a relationship the kind of commitment I think you'd want."

Sudden anger spurted through Marisol. It was almost welcome, making her feel less numb, more alive. "Oh no, Alex. That's not it. It's not that you doubt what you can bring to a relationship. You doubt me. You don't trust women!"

He stared at her.

"No," he said, his voice hoarse. "That's not so. I don't want to hurt you—"

"It is true," she continued, her voice rising. "I'm not like Juanita, Alex. Or Irena, either," she added as a sudden wind gusted.

"I didn't say you were," he protested.

"But you're thinking it, aren't you?" Even as he

shook his head, she knew it was the truth. Alex didn't trust women. He didn't trust *her*. And he couldn't see it.

Tears pricked her eyes as her anger seeped slowly out of her, replaced by frustration and sadness. Was he going to walk away from everything they had? Their growing relationship?

Her love?

"Alex, I think we should give this relationship a chance," she said, trying to sound logical. "You may find you're worried for no reason."

She saw doubt and hesitation on his face, and knew he wouldn't agree. He didn't believe in her.

"I . . ." He stopped. "I've wrestled with this for days. I don't think I can."

"You mean you don't want to," she shot back, anger returning to bubble in her again. "You think all women are like Juanita. But we're not. *I'm not.*"

She looked away, fighting tears, the coffee-flavored ice cream now tasting like dust in her mouth. She took a deep breath, then turned back to Alex.

He was staring at her, his expression sad and guilty.

So this was it. He'd made up his mind.

She felt as deflated as an old balloon. "Maybe you better take me home now."

He nodded.

They were silent on the ride home. Marisol wanted to cry, but she forced herself not to.

As they neared her home, he turned to her. "I'm sorry, Marisol. More than you know."

She looked at him and recognized the turmoil on his face.

"Maybe—maybe if you give me some time . . ." His voice faded. "Why don't we—talk—in a few weeks?"

"All right." Her voice came out scratchy. He pulled into her driveway, and she practically leaped out of the car. "Good-bye."

It sounded so final as she ran up the steps to her home.

Chapter Eleven

Marisol let herself in, not looking back when Alex called softly after her, *"Hasta la vista."* Until we see each other again . . . Ha! she thought, her keys rattling in her shaking hand. If she ever looked at him again . . .

She almost sagged with relief when she saw everyone was in the kitchen. Calling out hello, she ran up the stairs to the bathroom she shared with Christa. She needed time to compose herself.

There, she quietly let the tears come, not crying as hard as she wanted, afraid her family would hear her. Then she splashed cold water on her face. She was growing angry again. How could Alex possibly believe she was anything like Juanita? Or Irena either, although Irena had, at least, acted out of love—her love for Leo. At least Marisol hoped so.

But Juanita was a cold, calculating woman, and had

hurt Alex deeply—more than Marisol had realized. But she would never act like Juanita. Ever!

She managed to pull herself together, then left the bathroom, pasting a smile on her stiff face.

"Marisol, come downstairs as soon as you can!" Christa's voice shrilled up the stairs. "*Mamita* has an announcement!"

Marisol walked slowly down, forcing herself to smile, and dutifully appeared in the kitchen.

Her parents, Christa, and *Mamita* were gathered around the table, with *Mamita's* friend, Manuel.

"I have good news!" her grandmother burst out as soon as Marisol appeared.

"Yes?" Marisol asked. Had her grandmother won the lottery?

"Manuel and I are getting married!" She and Manuel both beamed.

Marisol gasped. She hadn't seen that coming. But how wonderful for her grandmother and Manuel!

"*Mamita!* How super!" she cried, and flung her arms around her grandmother to hug her. Margarita squeezed her back, and then of course she had to hug Manuel, and then everyone in her family was hugging everyone else.

"I told everyone just a few minutes ago—I didn't think you'd be back so soon, I was planning to tell you when you got home," her grandmother was saying. "Oh, *niña,* you are crying!"

"From happiness," Marisol declared, brushing away the tears spilling down. There was no reason to let anyone suspect they were anything but tears of joy. She certainly didn't want to spoil *Mamita*'s happy surprise with her own problems.

But she knew the tears were partly for herself.

Her grandmother was so happy. If only she could be too!

Alex slid into the booth opposite Pablo at the sandwich place where they frequently ate, located between his home and Pablo's.

"What a week," he said to his cousin, opening up his wrapped sandwich. "I'm glad it's Friday—I'm beat."

"You look it." Pablo studied him for a moment and Alex, uncomfortable, dropped his gaze to his chicken parmiginia sandwich.

It wasn't just his hectic schedule while they were short-handed at work. Tomorrow, fortunately, his coworker would be back and then the ER doctors could go back to a more normal routine—not counting summer vacations and other emergencies that were sure to happen. At least next week promised to be a more normal one.

He could handle that—he had before. If he could manage an internship at a big city hospital, he could deal with being temporarily overworked at a small hospital.

But added to that, he hadn't slept well for almost a week . . . since the day Pablo's traitorous girlfriend eloped with Leo. The day he'd began having serious doubts about his relationship with Marisol.

He looked up to see Pablo staring at him.

"Yeah, I'm tired. I've put in a lot of hours and I haven't slept particularly well this week," he admitted.

He figured his cousin would echo his words. Pablo probably wasn't sleeping well either. He'd been really anxious to get together and speak to Alex.

But his cousin's next words surprised him. "I've been sleeping great."

"You have?" Alex asked. He paused, his sandwich halfway to his mouth. He observed his cousin. He did look well-rested, surprisingly.

"Yeah." Pablo smiled suddenly. "Since a couple of days after Irena eloped with Leo. I feel—you won't believe this, but I feel like a weight has been lifted off me!"

"You do?" Alex couldn't contain his astonishment.

"Yes. At first, I was upset. Then, I realized—are you ready for this? That I felt *relieved!*" Pablo grinned, then took a bite of his roast beef sandwich.

"Relieved?" Alex echoed, knowing he sounded like a parrot.

"Yes, relieved. Listen, Alex, you know I haven't been too happy with Irena. The day she eloped, I was seriously thinking of going over there and telling her I wanted to call off our engagement. I just couldn't see us married to each other. I thought she'd be devastated, and I put it off, and was trying to think of how to tell her, and whether I should do it that night. Then she eloped with Leo."

"Saving you the trouble of ending it," Alex said, still shocked. Although he shouldn't be, he thought. He'd even advised his cousin to put on the brakes and reconsider his intention to marry Irena.

"Exactly. But at first I was just—shocked, I guess, in a daze. And maybe a little hurt that it came from her and not me. And that she didn't have the decency to tell me in person; she just ran away." Pablo shrugged. "But in the end, it was exactly right for me. We wouldn't have been happy together. I'm convinced of it now."

"Well." Alex blew out a breath. "Then I am happy for you, because it's worked out so well."

"Yes, and—even better," he smiled again, wider this time. "I realized something else. I never loved Irena. It was a convenient relationship, that's all. I mean, we were fighting more and more about everything. Like the day we ate dinner at Marisol's house. We'd had a big blowup about where we were going on our honeymoon."

"Oh."

"I realized what love really is because I'm feeling it—for Celia," Pablo concluded.

"Oh." Alex repeated, staring at Pablo, who looked amazingly happy at that moment. "Are you sure? I mean, this just happened with Irena—"

"I was falling for Celia before that. I kept fighting it, since Irena and I were engaged, but deep inside I think I knew if I loved Irena I wouldn't have been thinking of Celia all the time, dreaming about her . . ." He gave Alex a smile that was definitely sappy.

Alex started. *He* kept thinking about Marisol, dreaming about *her*. But, he thought miserably, after last night she'd never speak to him again. "Well . . . should I congratulate you?" Alex asked cautiously, trying to push thoughts of Marisol aside for the moment so he could concentrate on his cousin.

"Not yet, but—I hope to speak to Celia this weekend.

She told me she doesn't want me on the rebound, and I understand that. But, hey, this isn't a rebound thing. I was falling for her while I was still engaged to Irena." Pablo bit into his sandwich with gusto.

"Well, then go after her," Alex said, his voice sounding strained.

Pablo shot him a suspicious look.

"You sound strange, Alejandro. What's up?" When Alex hesitated, Pablo probed further. "Something going on with you and Marisol?"

Alex chewed the delicious sandwich, then sipped his cola and sighed loudly. "Not much," he said sardonically.

"Meaning . . . ?" Pablo asked.

Alex sighed again.

"Tell me," Pablo commanded.

Alex told his cousin how, since Irena's elopement, he'd been very upset. How it had brought back memories of Juanita and her cheating. Pablo listened, his face grave, as Alex described how he realized he was moving too quickly with Marisol.

"I just don't think a relationship will work for me," Alex continued. "And I don't want to hurt her; she's a sweetheart, really, and she deserves better than a man who's going to string her along but not give her the commitment she wants and deserves."

Now Pablo looked astonished. "Why *wouldn't* you want a commitment with her?"

"I—well, I just don't think I'm the marrying type," Alex said. Pablo stared at him. "Maybe in the future— but not now."

"Do you love her?" Pablo demanded.

"Love? I don't know," Alex answered. Did he? He pictured Marisol. He cared about her, true, but love? He didn't know.

"Well, if you don't love her, of course you wouldn't want a commitment," Pablo said. "You wouldn't want to make the mistake I almost did!"

Alex nodded.

"But if you *do* love her"—Pablo leaned forward—"then don't let her get away! She's a great girl, Alex, and she seems so good for you. Don't let some stupid hang-up from the past get in your way."

"Stupid hang-up? I don't have—" Alex protested.

"Yes, you do," Pablo shot back. "Otherwise why are you obsessing about Juanita? That's in the past, man."

"But—" Alex stopped. He was at a loss for words. *Stupid hang-up?*

No, Pablo was wrong. He didn't have a stupid hang-up.

"I don't have any hang-ups," Alex said, enunciating slowly and carefully.

"No?" Pablo gave him a look. "I've seen the way Marisol looks at you. Why don't you try trusting her? And your own heart?"

Alex shook his head. "No. I'm trying to avoid further pain, not encourage it. For either of us."

"Stop being so stubborn. Give the relationship a chance," Pablo urged.

Still Alex balked at the idea. Why encourage Marisol and hurt her further? A long-term relationship wouldn't work.

"Think about it," Pablo said. "I'm going out with Celia tomorrow. I'll keep you informed about how it's going. And you think about what I said."

"Okay." Alex steered the conversation to baseball.

But driving home Pablo's words echoed.

Stupid hang-up?

Chapter Twelve

Marisol was glad to go to the library on Saturday. Normally she wasn't crazy about working on Saturdays on a beautiful summer day, even though she loved her job. Fortunately during July and August she wasn't scheduled to work too many Saturdays. But this particular weekend she was glad to escape the house.

So far, everyone was paying so much attention to *Mamita* and her surprising news that no one had noticed she was down in the dumps. Christa had given her a long look last night, though, when she answered her cousin's question and said she wasn't seeing Alex this weekend. She left it at that, hoping people would assume he was working. But she was sure the questions would start soon.

She spent some time checking her summer reading plans for the next two weeks' activities, then looked over the returned books, getting an idea of what the younger patrons were reading. Joyce didn't work weekends, so she had Mandy, the teenager who worked part time, shelve the books, and got started on her orders for the fall.

Raised voices from the main room drifted toward her. She opened up a catalog as she heard them grow closer.

"There she is," a woman said in Spanish.

Marisol looked up.

Leo's parents were bearing down on her.

Leo's parents? *Here?*

She stared in surprise, straightening in her seat, as she observed Mrs. Sanchez's angry expression. Mr. Sanchez looked disturbed, his face pale.

"What do you have to say for yourself?" Mrs. Sanchez demanded in English as she reached Marisol's desk.

"What do you mean?" asked Marisol, confused. What was she talking about?

Mrs. Sanchez's cheeks were red. "You should be ashamed!" she declared loudly.

Marisol raised her eyebrows, feeling the beginnings of anger. Why were they marching in here trying to start trouble?

"I don't know what you're talking about," she said.

"I'm talking about you! And Leo! And that—that—" Mrs. Sanchez switched to Spanish. "That woman!" Then she added a nasty word.

Marisol stood up, staring at Leo's mother. Had she gone off the deep end?

Mandy had sidled up to the desk, her stance defensive.

"What do you mean? And lower your voice—this is a library," Marisol said coldly, dropping hers.

"I'll speak any way I want to," the woman snapped. "You witch! You set this up!"

"What?" Marisol was astounded. "What are you talking about?"

"You strung him along when you never wanted to marry my son! Then you set him up with that woman— you knew what she's like—and she tricked Leo and brainwashed him and made him elope with her!"

Marisol almost fell back into her seat, she was so shocked. Leo's parents thought she had set Leo up with Irena? They thought the elopement was her fault?

"That's absolutely ridiculous!" she exclaimed, then, switching to Spanish also, she continued, "Your son and I were just friends, nothing more. I didn't introduce him to Irena, they met in dance class. And I had no idea they were seeing each other until I heard that they eloped!"

"It was your class!" Mrs. Sanchez screamed.

By now several patrons had drawn close, whether because they were curious or they were afraid for Marisol, she was unsure. From nearby Marisol heard the voice of Pat, one of the women who worked here.

"You'll have to leave immediately," Pat said firmly to Mrs. Sanchez as she drew closer. "We can't have anyone in here making a scene."

Mrs. Sanchez sent her a nasty look. "I'll make a scene if I want to. This woman has ruined my son's life—and mine too."

"That's not true," Marisol protested hotly. "If Leo

chose to marry a woman he met in my class, that's *his* choice. Not mine or anyone else's."

"It's your fault!" Mrs. Sanchez exclaimed as her husband tugged on her arm suddenly. He was beginning to look remorseful, finally aware his wife was creating a major scene.

She switched back to English. "You're going to pay for this!"

"Maybe, Olga—" Mr. Sanchez began.

She shook off her husband's hand.

"I'm calling the police!" Pat declared. "You can't come in here and threaten—"

"You better leave," Marisol told them, "before the police get here!" Her hands began to tremble with her anger. How dare they come into the place where she worked and accuse her of setting Leo and Irena up? "If you're upset, go talk to Leo!"

Pat picked up the phone and dialed as Mandy drew closer to Marisol.

"We should go," Mr. Sanchez said, attempting to pull his wife.

"I'm not going anywhere!" she shouted.

Pat said in a clear voice, "I want to report that there's a woman in the library, making terroristic threats against one of our employees and creating a disturbance." There was a pause, and then Pat continued, "I believe the employee can identify who she is." She stared at Mrs. Sanchez.

"Olga, come!" her husband said, and this time he pulled her hard.

She stumbled slightly, then glared at Marisol. "Just wait till Leo gets back with that woman!"

"I look forward to it!" Marisol snapped. "I believe they'll be very happy, and I want to wish them well!" She gave the venomous woman her biggest smile.

"You go, girl," Mandy said.

Mr. Sanchez practically dragged his wife out of the library. She cursed loud enough for the patrons to hear as she left.

Marisol sank into her seat, her legs trembling.

Thank goodness Mrs. Sanchez wasn't her mother-in-law!

Alex dropped wearily into his favorite chair and stretched out his legs. His stomach grumbled. It had been a long time since lunch, but at the moment all he wanted to do was sit.

It was almost eight P.M. on Sunday, and he'd ended up working extra hours because the day's hundred-degree, sticky weather had brought in loads of people suffering from sunburns, heat exhaustion, and breathing problems. There'd been two bad car accidents in the area as well, with injured adults and children. Things had finally slowed down and he and Dr. Rhastogi, who'd also worked overtime, had finally been able to leave by seven thirty

Despite his being tired, he'd been glad to immerse himself in work. It kept his mind off of Marisol and the overwhelming feelings of desire and confusion and guilt that were constantly bombarding him.

Now, without distractions, it was hard to keep her from his thoughts.

His stomach grumbled again, and he considered calling for take-out pizza. That would probably take too long, he decided. He should have picked one up or gotten a sandwich. Well, he'd just have to make something. He was about to get out of the chair when the phone rang.

He looked at the caller ID, hoping maybe it would be Marisol. Although he knew she would have no reason to call him, still, the illogical hope wedged inside him.

The number was Pablo's.

He picked it up. "Hey, Pablo."

"Hey, Alejandro," Pablo responded. "Want to hear something interesting?" His cousin sounded excited, almost amused.

"I could use it."

Pablo began to speak rapidly. "You won't believe this. Leo Sanchez's parents went down to the library where Marisol works and harassed and threatened her."

"They *what*?" Alex exclaimed, sitting bolt upright in his chair.

"They harassed her. Leo's mother accused Marisol of getting Leo and Irena together on purpose, and said it was all her fault they eloped. Do you believe that? And then she threatened Marisol."

"Threatened her? Is she all right?" He had a death grip on the phone.

"Yes, but I hear she's upset."

"Who wouldn't be? Did she call the police?" Alex asked.

"Yeah, but when they got there Leo's parents had already left. The library staff reported the incident, though. I think they're afraid it could happen again."

A panicky feeling welled up in Alex. He pictured Marisol facing Leo's nasty parents.

"Did the police arrest them?"

"I think they gave them some kind of warning since this was the first time anything like this happened. Those details are unclear."

Alex paused. "Did Marisol tell you all this?" She should have called him, not Pablo. Despite everything, he would have been there for her.

"No." Pablo's voice had an odd note.

"How did you hear about it?"

"Marisol's grandmother, Margarita, and her cousin, Christa, called me."

"They did?" Alex felt confusion. Why would they—

"Supposedly, it was so I could let Irena know when she returns from her honeymoon. Margarita said that she thinks Irena could be their next target, and she didn't know Irena's phone number. But—" He stopped.

"But what?" Alex asked.

"But . . . I think there's more to it than that."

"Go on," Alex urged.

Pablo chuckled. "I have a feeling they wanted me to tell *you*."

"Oh. Why?"

"Maybe they think Marisol's too embarrassed or upset to tell you."

Or maybe they suspect something's not right between

Marisol and me, and she won't tell me her problems, Alex thought. A wave of guilt flashed through him, intense and painful. If he had been a better person, a good friend, a true boyfriend, wouldn't she have come to him with this distressing situation and asked his advice?

"This is terrible," he said, his voice coming out raspy. "How could they give her such a hard time when it was their own son who eloped? Poor Marisol. She doesn't deserve that kind of treatment!"

"I had a feeling you'd think that way," Pablo said lightly. "So . . . what are you going to do?"

Alex knew immediately, had known since Pablo first described the incident.

"I'm going to talk to Leo's parents and set them straight."

While at work the following morning, Alex kept thinking about Marisol and how Leo's parents—mostly his mom, according to Pablo—had threatened her.

Pablo had been supportive of Alex's plan to speak to Mr. and Mrs. Sanchez. He'd also promised to let Irena know when she returned.

"You should call Marisol," he had urged Alex.

But Alex didn't think that was a good idea. "No, she's probably upset, and I don't want her to know what I'm planning. I'm sure she'd say to forget it. And I don't want to forget it."

But after he'd gotten off the phone, ate a sandwich, showered, and fell into bed, he couldn't sleep right away. Despite his fatigue, he kept thinking about the situation.

He wanted to call Marisol and offer support. But he was sure the call would be unwelcome.

Fortunately, after putting in a lot of overtime during the last week, he didn't have to work a full day on Monday. He was back home and able to relax by two in the afternoon.

By three he was anxious to go over to see the Sanchezes.

But they probably would be at work, so he caught up on errands and then went out for an early dinner of pizza with one of his friends from the hospital.

By seven thirty he headed over to the Sanchez house. Pablo had given him the address in Roxbury, and he had no trouble finding the small but neat-looking home.

Lights were on, and he rang the doorbell. The door was opened by a gray-haired man in his fifties.

"Can I help you?" he asked Alex.

"Mr. Sanchez? I'm Dr. Alejandro Lares." His title often impressed people, and he had no compunctions about using it for that purpose now. "I'd like to talk to you and your wife about Leo and Irena—and Marisol."

Mr. Sanchez blanched. "I . . . uh . . . ," he stuttered.

"Who is that?" came a whiny-sounding voice from inside.

"Dr. Alejandro Lares," Alex called before Leo's father could say anything.

Leo's mother, a trim woman with short brown hair, appeared by the door, her eyebrows raised.

"I'd like to talk to you both about Leo, Irena, and Marisol," Alex repeated.

"About—" Her face flushed suddenly, and an angry expression replaced her surprised one. "About that woman?"

"Can I come in?" Alex forced himself to speak politely. He wondered if "that woman" referred to Irena or Marisol. "I'm Pablo Lares' cousin—Pablo is the man Irena was supposed to marry."

"Come in," Mr. Sanchez said, opening the door.

Mrs. Sanchez stood aside, looking mutinous.

Alex entered, and Mr. Sanchez led him to the living room, which was decorated in gold and cream. He recognized, from working at his father's store when he was a teenager, that the furniture was cheap and gaudy. It looked so pristine that he knew the room was rarely used.

Mr. Sanchez sat on a couch by the window and Mrs. Sanchez indicated a chair across from him, then switched on the light by the chair. Alex sat, feeling like a patient about to undergo surgery, with the operating light shining down.

Mrs. Sanchez sat on the couch beside her husband.

"I came tonight to talk to you about your son and Irena," he began without preamble, wanting to get quickly to the point.

"What about them?" Mrs. Sanchez snapped.

"No one knew they were going out—not Irena's fiancé, my cousin Pablo. Not their families, obviously— no one," he continued. "Not even the people in the salsa class, who they socialized with—"

"That teacher, Marisol, knew," Mrs. Sanchez said harshly. "Leo's known her for over a year—"

"No," Alex said firmly. "She didn't. *No one knew.*"

"She did!" Mrs. Sanchez exclaimed. "She pushed them together! She was stirring up trouble! I never liked her. The first time I met her I knew she thought she was too good for Leo. I said to my husband, mark my words, that girl is trouble! And see, I was right!" She shot her husband a look. "All she wanted was to create problems for Leo. She set him up with that—that Irena!"

"That's not true!" Alex declared, amazed at the woman's venomous attack. "She certainly had no reason to push them together—and she didn't. I'm in the salsa class too—I saw what happened. Pablo and Irena had been growing apart. No one pushed Leo and Irena together—least of all Marisol. And she's *not* the kind who thinks she's better than others. She's a very caring person—"

"That girl is a troublemaker! She can't be trusted!"

"Olga—" Her husband interrupted, looking uncomfortable. Alex wondered if he was beginning to realize that his wife was getting carried away.

"Trouble, trouble, trouble!" she exclaimed, standing up and waving her hands dramatically.

Alex found himself rising too. "No," he insisted, fighting to sound calm. "She's not a troublemaker! She wants people to get along and she wants the best for everyone." He felt his chest tightening in a peculiar way as he said the words. "She is trustworthy. She'd never hurt anyone. I'd trust her with my life."

As he said the words, they seemed to reverberate in

his head, bouncing back and forth like an echo in the hospital halls. *She is trustworthy . . . I'd trust her with my life . . .*

He swallowed.

Marisol *was* trustworthy.

And he *would* trust her with his life.

Marisol was a kind, sweet, genuine person. As well as being beautiful and fun to be around.

Most of all, she *was* a trustworthy person.

He knew it deep down in his bones. The truth flowed through every cell in his body.

Why hadn't he realized it before?

The knowledge seemed to course inside him, like his very bloodstream.

He would trust Marisol with his life.

The Sanchezes were staring at him. Belatedly he realized Mrs. Sanchez had said something.

"What did you say?" he asked, his tone quieter.

"You can't trust her," Mrs. Sanchez said.

"Yes I can," Alex shot back, "and so can everyone with half a brain. I've never met a more special person. Leo is lucky she's his friend."

Mrs. Sanchez opened her mouth, but Alex cut in.

"You were out of line when you went to the library. I don't ever want to hear that you're threatening her again." His voice was cool and controlled. "Stay away from her, or I will not only go to the police, I'll go to my friend who's a lawyer."

Mrs. Sanchez's face turned red. "Get out of my house!" she cried.

"Gladly." Alex moved toward the door. "And I doubt if Leo would be happy to hear about your behavior. It's embarrassing."

"Get out!"

"Olga—"

She shook off her husband's hand.

"He's right about Leo," Mr. Sanchez said.

Alex had already reached the door and pulled it open as he heard Mrs. Sanchez exclaim, "That's not true!"

He was relieved to leave the heated atmosphere of the house.

As he strode toward his car, something inside of him was singing. *Marisol is trustworthy! I'd trust her with my life!*

An overwhelming desire to see Marisol, and tell her his realization, engulfed him.

He stopped short when he reached his car.

He'd pushed Marisol away. He'd practically told her he didn't think they had a future together.

His heart constricted. What had he done?

He got into the car and began driving. But instead of driving home, he found himself going past the library where Marisol worked. Impulsively he got out and went in. It was quiet, with only a few patrons gazing at books. The librarian on duty said Marisol wasn't in on Monday nights.

Alex got back into his car and drove aimlessly. He passed the movie theater on the opposite side of the highway, where they'd been less than two weeks ago, and the shopping center where they'd walked and he'd kissed her. He continued up the highway, passing the ice cream place where they'd sat and she'd dejectedly picked at her ice cream.

Dios. It was his fault she'd been upset. Had he broken her heart?

His own heart squeezed harder as it occurred to him that she might want nothing to do with him now.

No. *No!* It couldn't be too late . . . could it?

He knew now that she was trustworthy. She was the best woman he'd ever met. He never wanted—

He never wanted to let her go. He wanted to be with her, always.

He loved her.

It was as if Marisol's sunshiny smile warmed him. He felt a wave of happiness and warmth. He loved Marisol!

He realized with a start that he was heading away from home, and drove up the highway, still thinking fast and furiously.

What if she didn't feel the same way he did?

Thinking back on their last few weeks together, the time they'd spent with each other, he suspected she had fallen in love with him too.

But since he'd pushed her away . . . would her love survive that?

He needed to see her, talk to her.

A glance at the clock showed him it was eight thirty.

There was no place to turn here, so he went up to a large shopping center, drove in, and turning the car around, drove back toward Dover.

He didn't call, afraid that Marisol would tell him not to come over. When he pulled up to her house it was after nine.

The room upstairs was dark. In fact, in the house, only the living room light appeared to be on. He could see Marisol's parents, sitting and watching TV, through the window. Maybe she'd gone to bed early, or she wasn't home.

He needed to think about how to approach her. How to ask her to forgive him for being so thickheaded. He continued up the street and turned to drive toward Pablo's house.

What he needed, he thought, was a grand gesture. Something romantic. He definitely had to bounce the idea forming in his brain off of someone—and his cousin lived only a few minutes away.

He was not going to lose Marisol. He was going to show her that he did trust her. That he loved her!

Chapter Thirteen

Tuesday morning was busy at the library—and Marisol was very glad.

She'd gone to the movies last night with her cousin, anxious to get out and get her mind off of Alex. The action adventure they'd seen had been entertaining, but once home, she had been restless and sad.

Christa was the only one who had noticed her despondent mood, and Marisol had answered her cousin's questions with the statement that she wasn't sure if she was going to keep seeing Alex. For once Christa didn't ask her anything more, just gave her a long, sympathetic look, then a sudden hug.

"Whatever you do will be right," she'd said.

Her work had been an escape, and the day started out so busy she'd hardly had a moment to think about lost loves or anything else. There were a large number of children present for the reading program. After she'd read the story about a dragon and a princess, they'd made the dragon puppets. With glue sticking to little fingers and sparkles flying, she and the two teens helping her could barely keep up. She enjoyed the work but she was relieved when the last of the children left.

"Wow, that was harder than I thought," Mandy said.

"And we still have to clean up!" Liz chimed in.

"I'll help too," Joyce said, coming up behind them. She'd been busy at the front desk, since many of the mothers were checking out books, but she was available now.

"Let's get it over with then," Marisol suggested.

Between the four of them, the cleanup didn't take as long as she'd anticipated, and they were done a little after twelve. The girls, who worked only part time, left, and seeing the area was quiet Marisol told Joyce she was going to eat lunch.

She grabbed a travel book and retreated to the staff area with the lunch she'd packed. Now she did have time to think of Alex.

She sighed. She missed him—his smile, his wry sense of humor, his caring manner.

She wondered for the thousandth time if she should just go on seeing him but with the idea of expecting no commitment and no future. But she didn't think she could stand that. She loved him. She wanted to marry him.

If only he would change his mind about their relationship. If only she could convince him to trust and give love a chance!

She tried to shove him from her mind, and, pushing aside her sandwich temporarily, she opened the book.

It had occurred to her last night that maybe she and Celia should get away. A nice trip, something fun—maybe with some sightseeing—would get their minds off of men in general. Off of two particular men who were cousins.

She leafed through the book. Italy—that would be fun. But it also sounded romantic. So did France and Spain.

She'd always wanted to visit Egypt and see the pyramids. But she didn't know if she had enough money saved for a big trip like that.

If she visited Puerto Rico she'd have to spend time with her relatives there, and she didn't think she wanted to do that. She continued to flip through the book. Parts of Canada looked interesting, and that wasn't too far away . . .

She finished up her lunch and determined to speak to Celia about a trip after class tonight.

Joyce went to lunch, and Marisol saw that a stack of books had been returned. She had some free time, so she went through them, making mental notes as to which books were the most popular and went out again and again.

She paused at one of her favorites, *The Little Engine That Could.* Impulsively, she picked it up and retreated to her desk.

This had always been a personal favorite of hers since her mother had read it to her as a child. The story of the brave train going up the hill, trying mightily to pull its load, never failed to touch her. She could hear the train saying, "I think I can, I think I can."

A sudden frisson of excitement shot up her spine. *I think I can.*

Positive thinking—like the train. She could do that. Yes, she could!

I think I can, I think I can, reverberated through her head. She could convince Alex. She could make him see that they were meant to be together. That he could trust her, trust the idea of love.

It might not be easy. But, given the chance, she was positive she could make him see the light. That love was a wonderful thing, and that he could love and be loved.

Why hadn't she been more positive before? She wasn't one to give up easily. She'd been so surprised by Alex's idea that they should put the brakes on their relationship, so disturbed—she must have been in shock or something. But now she was ready, and willing, to fight for their relationship, for their future.

She reread the book quickly, and shut it carefully.

She was going to win over Alex.

She couldn't wait to see him again.

Class tonight was hours away. It was only one forty-five but she got out at four today, so maybe . . .

She quickly formulated a plan.

The moment she left work, Marisol drove to the condo complex where she knew Alex lived. Driving around in the late-afternoon shimmering sunshine, she couldn't find his car. She wasn't be surprised—she knew he often worked on Tuesdays. And she wouldn't disturb him at work.

Impatient to see him, she drove quickly home. She'd already planned her outfit for tonight's class. She prayed he'd be there, but if he wasn't, she was determined to go to his place and see him afterward.

Her family was still busy talking about *Mamita*'s upcoming wedding, which was planned for a Sunday afternoon in September. Marisol ate a small, quick dinner and excused herself early to shower and get ready for class.

While she was getting dressed in her favorite red dress, Christa entered the room.

"You look great in that," her cousin remarked, studying Marisol. "You also seem a lot happier than you did last night."

"I am," Marisol cofirmed. "I'll tell you about it later, okay?"

Christa gave her the thumbs-up sign, then flipped open her cell phone and called a friend.

Marisol spent extra time on her makeup and then realized with a start she was running a little late. She drove as fast as she could to the studio, and entered through the back, as usual. The tap class didn't meet during the summer but she was in the habit of entering that way.

As soon as she was in the back area, Celia came flying out of the main room.

"Marisol!"

Seeing her friend's happy face, Marisol stopped short.

"Qué pasa?" she asked lightly. Only one thing would make Celia look so ecstatic.

Celia grabbed her hands. "Marisol, Pablo came to see me over the weekend! And we've been going out! I didn't have a chance to call you sooner because we were talking so late last night—and I had a busy day at work—" Her smile was wide as her words tumbled out.

"Yes?" Marisol asked, gripping Celia's hands.

"He's spent the whole last week thinking. And he realized—he said his feelings for me were much stronger than his feelings ever were for Irena, and he realized that meant he loved me!" she finished with a squeal. "He loves *me!*"

"Oh Celia!" Marisol hugged her friend. "I'm so happy for you!"

"And I told him I love him too," Celia continued, almost dancing. "Oh, I'm babbling, I know, but—I'm so happy!"

They hugged again. Marisol felt gladness for Celia—and Pablo—sweep through her.

And hope quickly followed. Maybe if Pablo had come to this realization, then Alex would follow . . . ?

"Marisol? Celia?" Sondra's voice echoed from the storage room. She emerged, smiling. "Can you help me set up?"

They got busy, and Marisol noted that Celia's steps were light and confident.

She tried to adopt the same attitude, but she felt a little anxiety as they unlocked the front door. Within five minutes, the students began to gather—Anne and Dominick, Stella, and Xavier and Shannon entered the room.

As more of the students filed in, it hit Marisol again that this was the second-to-last class.

She hoped Alex would be here.

It was almost time to start. She was by the CD player with Sondra when she heard a murmur, and someone whistled.

Glancing up, she saw Pablo and Alex entering the room.

She hardly looked at Pablo, although he was dressed formally like Alex.

Alex commanded her attention. Dressed in a black suit, with a starkly white shirt and vibrant red tie, he looked devastatingly handsome. Like every woman's dream man—dark and gorgeous and dressed to kill.

She almost gasped.

She saw his eyes sweep the room and stop as they met her gaze.

Slowly, he smiled.

And Marisol melted.

Alex couldn't help feeling a little nervous as he took his place in line with the other students in the class.

He'd made his plans carefully, coordinating with Pablo. They'd called Sondra to ensure her cooperation too.

But the minute he saw Marisol he felt like most of his thoughts flew out of his head.

She looked absolutely beautiful. Stylish and sensual

and sleek in a red dress, her lovely face framed by her gorgeous, wavy dark hair, she looked like the kind of woman every man dreamed of. And the minute she met his look and gave her radiant smile, he knew he would never love anyone else. Had really never loved anyone else.

There was only Marisol.

Xavier stepped beside him, startling him back to reality. He quickly followed the moves with the others, forcing himself to pay attention to what Sondra was saying.

They went through the motions of the salsa, reviewing all the steps they'd learned so far, and then repeating the process with the music. He kept his eyes on Marisol at the front of the room, as she swayed to the music.

When Sondra divided them up, he found himself partnered with Shannon.

"You look very nice tonight!" she said brightly. "You and your cousin." She grinned. "Although I suspect this isn't just for the class; it's for Marisol and Celia, right?"

He grinned but didn't answer her question. "Thank you," he said simply.

As they went through the motions of dancing, he wished he could simply fast-forward to the end of class. When he could be with Marisol, talk to her, as he planned.

During the class's first break, several people surrounded both Celia and Marisol, asking questions. By the time it was the second break he pushed forward, anxious to get at least one word with her.

"Hi," she said to him, giving him her bright smile.

"Hi," he answered. "You look sensational—"

Stella had approached, and observed, "You both look great! Now, Marisol, I have a question—"

There went any opportunity to say something about seeing her later.

Within minutes, they were back to dancing.

He kept his eye on the clock as they neared the end of class.

She loved the salsa class. She loved being one of the teachers. But if class didn't end soon, Marisol felt like she was going to jump out of her skin!

It was seven minutes to nine, and they were going to do the salsa one last time.

"We're back!" shrieked a triumphant voice.

Marisol whipped around in astonishment. That voice sounded like—

Irena and Leo entered the room with their arms around each other, smiling widely.

Gasps and exclamations followed their dramatic entrance.

Irena was dressed in a black skirt and white and black top she'd worn to class once before. She had never appeared so content, Marisol thought, staring at the couple.

Leo, dressed in khakis and a dark green shirt, looked more relaxed than Marisol had ever seen him.

The two of them actually looked very happy!

Someone started clapping, and Marisol found herself joining in as others followed.

"Welcome back!" Stella exclaimed as several people shouted, "Congratulations!"

People rushed toward the newlyweds, who began hugging those nearby.

Marisol glanced at Pablo. He was smiling as if he was genuinely pleased. She saw no trace of jealousy in his expression. As she watched, he turned and looked toward Celia, and winked at her.

Thank goodness! Marisol thought, letting out a breath. She moved to join the group surrounding Irena and Leo.

"Congratulations!" she said, hugging them in turn.

After another minute Irena held a hand up.

"We have an announcement," she proclaimed.

Sondra was clapping her hands. "Let's listen, everyone!" she urged. Her smile made Marisol suspect she had known all along the newlyweds would be appearing.

The class quieted, and Irena spoke up. "We're married, and Las Vegas was fabulous. But we know our families and friends were disappointed that they missed out on our wedding. So—we're going to have a church ceremony and the reception I planned to have originally." She turned to look at Pablo.

There was silence. Pablo, though, was smiling and nodding.

"I spoke to Pablo and he had no objection," Irena continued, smiling back. Then she turned to Leo, and her gentle smile startled Marisol. It seemed that Irena was really in love with Leo. "And Leo agrees."

There were murmurs throughout the room.

"And the best part is—" Irena threw her hands wide—"you're all invited!"

At this everyone burst into applause. Marisol clapped with them, but found herself looking for Alex, now that the shock of seeing Irena and Leo was wearing off.

He was standing near Pablo, clapping as enthusiastically as everyone else. He seemed to feel her gaze and turned to meet her look, smiling.

He had known about this, she realized. Pablo must have said something.

But everyone else was surprised and delighted. She certainly was. And she was happy that Leo seemed to have found the right woman, and that Irena was happy too.

When it quieted, Sondra exclaimed, "And of course we'll all do the salsa!"

Laughter, exclamations, and more clapping met her words.

"Well, class is almost over," Sondra declared. "Next week is our last class—so what do you say we practice one more time?"

They all agreed, and Sandra directed them back to the places where they'd stood when Leo and Irena arrived. She had the newlyweds move to the front.

Marisol had been partnered with Stella, and when the music began they danced with the others. She tried not to watch what Alex, who was partnered with Celia, was doing, but she couldn't help stealing a glance when the opportunity arose.

The class, she thought proudly, was doing well. They'd learned a lot in seven weeks.

The music ended, and people began applauding again. Marisol couldn't wait till everyone left.

But they didn't. People lingered, speaking to Irena and Leo, slowly—too slowly!—leaving the studio. After nearly fifteen minutes, in which Marisol smiled and nodded and said good-bye to one person after another, Sondra briskly approached the newlyweds.

"Now, go home and have some romantic time alone!" she declared, making shooing motions. "We have to clean up here."

"Oh! Sorry," Irena said. "I was just describing the chapel in Las Vegas." She sent an apologetic glance around. "Come on, dear, let's let them get out of here," she finished, tugging on Leo's hand.

He sent her a bemused look. "Of course. Bye!" he said, and let her lead him out. Shannon and Xavier, Anne and Dominick, and three more straggling students followed.

Marisol glanced to her left. Alex and Pablo were still standing there behind her, Sondra, and Celia.

"Now," Sondra said as the last student departed. "Celia and Marisol, these nice guys volunteered to help you straighten and lock up. I'm leaving." She smiled, waved, and left the room. Seconds later they heard the door shut.

Marisol stared at Alex.

"Before we help straighten up, may I have this dance?"

Alex asked in formal tones. He took Marisol's hand and bowed.

Confusion swept through her. Dance? What did he mean? But she saw Celia move to the stereo, and realized this must have been prearranged.

As she watched, Pablo sidled up to Celia and whispered something to her, and then they assumed their positions for the salsa.

Marisol turned back to stare at Alex. He was smiling at her.

"Salsa with me," he said softly. "Yes?"

"Yes," she murmured, and let him lead her to the middle of the dance floor.

They began the steps, Alex dancing in his careful way. As the music flowed around them, he relaxed a little, and Marisol felt some of her own tension drain. She remembered thinking not long ago that she wished they could dance together like this all the time.

"We dance well together, don't we?" Alex whispered, echoing her thoughts.

Celia and Pablo had moved into a corner, and must have dimmed the lights, because all of a sudden it was darker in the room. Alex pulled her a little closer.

"Yes," Marisol whispered back. And then she couldn't stop herself. "Alex, I need to talk to you—"

"Shh." He moved his hand and pressed a finger to her lips. "Not until I have a chance to talk to you first." He whirled her around. "After our dance."

She sighed and decided to simply enjoy the moments in his arms. Talk could come later.

She thought she heard Celia and Pablo leaving the room.

As the last notes of the music echoed in the room, Alex pulled her closer still.

"Marisol." His lips were close to hers. His breath touched her face like a caress. She could smell his spicy aftershave.

Instinctively she tilted her face up to his.

"I have to apologize," he whispered, "but first—" and his lips swooped down on hers.

She barely had time to register his words. The minute his lips touched hers, sunshine burst through Marisol.

She wrapped her arms around him, and he squeezed her close. When their lips parted, he said her name in a breathless voice that made her shiver. And then he kissed her again and again.

Finally, he lifted his head, and she could only stare at his beloved face, feeling herself in a haze of sizzling contentment.

"I realized . . . I realized you are trustworthy," he said, clutching her tightly. "Marisol, I heard about what Leo's parents said to you at the library. I got so mad I went to see them—"

She started in surprise. "You did?"

"Yes, and I told them off. And when I was talking about you, it hit me—you're nothing like Juanita. You'd never be like her—you're a much better person. I'd trust you with my life."

Now she was trembling with happiness, feeling almost

giddy. "Oh Alex." She brushed her lips against his. "I'm so glad. Because I'd never let you down—"

"I know that," he said, smiling ruefully. "When I was busy defending you, I realized the truth of what I was saying. Can you forgive me for thinking otherwise?"

"Of course," she whispered, clinging to him.

"I'll never doubt you again." His eyes gleamed. And then, very softly, he said, "I love you, Marisol."

"Oh Alex!" She flung her arms around him. "I love you. I love you too!"

"Mi amor," he whispered. "My love." And then he kissed her again. "And just to prove to you how much I do trust you, and want you to be part of my life . . ." He smiled again, and suddenly dropped to one knee.

Marisol's heart flew into her throat. Was he about to do what she hoped . . . ?

In his formal attire, he looked not only masculine and handsome, but now so serious that she reached out and gently touched his face. Was he nervous? She wondered. Alex, the brilliant, handsome Latino man she'd always dreamed of, was uncertain about her?

"I love you, Marisol," he said huskily. "Please say you'll marry me and make me the happiest man in the entire world. Please say you'll share your life with me."

"Yes!" Marisol cried, and flung herself into his arms.

Alex gave a whoop that sounded totally unlike anything she'd heard from him and lifted her into the air. And then he whirled her around.

And Marisol felt completely and utterly happy.

Epilogue

"Everyone ready?" Irena asked in a low voice as she stood in her fancy white wedding gown.

There were nods and murmurs, and then Irena turned to the gathered guests.

"Now you will see a demonstration of salsa!" she proclaimed. She waved at the DJ, and within seconds hot salsa music slid from the speakers.

Marisol smiled up at Alex as they began to move in total sync. They'd practiced often, sometimes with Celia and Pablo, sometimes alone. The entire class was present at the wedding reception, including Sondra and her husband. And Marisol was proud to note that her students were dancing well.

Of course, some of them were quite obviously in love with their partners—Irena and Leo, Celia and Pablo,

Anne and Dominick—and Shannon and Xavier were plainly in love too.

And she knew that she and Alex positively glowed with the excitement of their love.

The wedding ceremony had been surprisingly delightful, though it was the second for Irena and Leo. Irena's parents were thrilled, and even Leo's parents appeared mollified. On the receiving line, Mrs. Sanchez had been civil to Marisol and Alex and Mr. Sanchez had gripped her hand hard when she offered her congratulations.

And the reception had been amazingly fun! With so many people she knew there, she'd known it would be a blast—but the best part of all was that she was there with Alex. And every touch and look was especially meaningful, because they were planning their own wedding now.

The dance had them turning, and she caught Celia's eye. Her friend smiled widely, sharing the same happiness that Marisol felt.

In a few months they'd be sharing more. Next May, they were having a double wedding!

Alex moved smoothly, and Marisol swayed in his arms, refocusing on his beloved face. She was so thrilled that they loved each other, and that she was going to be marrying the man she adored.

As they stepped in time to the music, Alex smiled down lovingly at her.

"We'll always dance the salsa together," he whispered.

"Always," Marisol answered, smiling.

And their hearts danced in time with the music.